Columbia Smoke

A Blue in Kamloops Novel

Alex McGilvery

Columbia Smoke
Alex McGilvery

ISBN 978-1-989092-53-8

Copyright Alex McGilvery 2021
Celticfrog Publishing
Kamloops, B.C.

Thanks to my editor Ann MacDonald, and my beta readers Eileen Bell, Elma Schemenauer, and Leo Tolstoy.

Chapter 1

Tuesday May 10

The alarm shrilled, and Blue sleepily wondered who was making toast in the middle of the night. The burnt smell made him cough.

"Blue!" Sam banged on the bedroom door. "There's a fire, we have to get out."

"Coming." Blue rolled out of bed, pulled clothes on, then fumbled his computer into its bag and slung it over his shoulder. He stuffed his phone into his pocket.

"Get a move on – there's smoke pouring in from the hall." Sam sounded nervous. When Blue opened the bedroom door, he saw the big man clutching a photo album; pictures from his trip to Japan last fall. The acrid stench of smoke made Blue cough. Between the shrill alarm and the smoke, he fought to remind himself this was no dream.

"Put it in my bag." Blue held it open.

"It's a fire we're supposed to leave everything and get out." Sam's eyes were wide.

"We have it now, don't worry about it." Blue yanked

the door to the balcony open and checked outside. "No smoke out here."

Sam joined him and slammed the door behind him. The thing stuck constantly. If they weren't on the third floor it would be a security risk. Below them a jet of flame came out of the wall.

"I'm not climbing down." Though he looked like a somewhat muscular Santa Claus, Sam was too smart to attempt the escape.

"Me neither." Blue pulled out his cell phone. Only twenty percent battery. He'd left the cord on the desk. The ones for the computer too. He was stuck with battery power for now. Too late to worry about it now. He dialed 911 and reported the fire, but sirens were already wailing as the fire truck approached.

The cheap plastic chair creaked as Sam lowered himself into it. "Might as well be comfortable while we wait."

Smoke drifted from under the balcony door, so Blue leaned against the dividing wall to the next apartment away from the door. The jet of flame roared like an engine

When the fire truck rolled up, someone got out and shone a flashlight along the building. Blue waved. The firefighters unhooked the ladder and got it extended. One climbed up to the balcony next door to Sam and Blue. They quickly dismantled the wall between the balconies.

"Anyone else in your apartment?"

"We're it. My daughter is away at school." Blue clutched the computer bag, but the firefighter didn't comment. She helped Sam onto the ladder and walked him

Columbia Smoke

down, then returned for Blue. Others helped him down from the truck as more examined the balcony for more people needing rescue.

From the ground across the alley, flames lit up the side of the building. Looked like three or four apartments on fire. Fire fighters had hoses connected and were spraying water on the flames.

He shivered and wished he'd thought to grab a jacket. With nothing else to do, Blue stood beside Sam and watched the firefighters work. The crowd on the ground grew, some people in light clothes, others with coats, and still others in pajamas.

People held onto cats, and dogs on leashes. One young woman guarded a stack of what looked like rabbit cages.

A woman danced in what could have been anything from rage to ecstasy, waving fists over her head. If she was saying anything, Blue couldn't hear it.

"Anybody got a light?" A young man holding a cigarette waved it about. Blue glanced over; he'd seen him in the entryway. The guy crashed in an apartment on the second floor.

"Over there." Someone pointed to the fire and people laughed. When Blue looked back to the fire, the woman had vanished.

Tenants clustered together and speculated about the cause or talked about what they would do now their homes were gone. Estimates of days, weeks, or even never, made the rounds as speculation about when they'd be able to get back in.

"Okay people." A woman with a clipboard waved for

attention. "Emergency Services is setting up at the Sportplex in MacArthur Island Park. If you can make your way over there, great. Otherwise a bus will be arriving to take you."

Blue and Sam made it onto the second bus trip to the arena, they were pointed to a room upstairs in the Sportsplex where they found coffee and cookies waiting for them.

Light was beginning to show in the east when a man in a firefighter's uniform came in and explained what Emergency Services was and how it would work. Inevitably it began with paperwork.

Blue sat down with a volunteer and filled out a form describing his housing situation and what his needs were. There was a voucher for temporary housing and one for clothes from Value Village. He had a paper to show for meals as well. Sam sat over two tables doing the same thing.

Blue was exhausted by the time the bus took them up to a motel on Columbia. This would be a new experience; he'd lived on the North Shore since he came to Kamloops.

Along with a few others, Blue was put into a tiny building with ten units. It formed a broken 'L' shape with the much newer two-storey building.

The room he was going to share with Sam had the usual two beds along with a rickety table and chairs. a tiny stove and bar fridge. An odd assortment of pots, pans, dishes and cutlery occupied the cupboards and drawers in the tiny kitchen. An odd musty smell made him remember visiting an old aunt when he was a kid, but it wasn't something he couldn't deal with.

Blue put the laptop on the table and connected it to the wifi. He'd have to find a power cord for it. Shouldn't be that hard.

He sent Molly a message. *Call me tonight.*

Blue lay on the bed closest to the window and stared at the ceiling. What should he do next? Getting to the North Shore to work would be a challenge, but not insurmountable. He'd have to buy a bus pass.

Sam walked in the door and plunked onto the other bed.

"My son wants me to fly out to Toronto and stay with them."

"Makes sense to at least visit. You did spend a month in Japan with your daughter."

"Yeah." Sam didn't sound convinced. "I don't want to desert you."

"If you were on your own, would you go?" Blue sat up and faced Sam.

"I would." Sam sighed and pulled out his phone, sent a text, then put it back in his pocket. "I will miss you."

"I hope so." Blue grinned at Sam's shocked expression, then they both laughed.

Sam's phone buzzed. He looked at it and rolled his eyes. "Eric has a flight for me leaving tomorrow. He works for WestJet, so he must have pulled some strings."

Blue pushed away the hollow feeling in his chest. Being alone without neither Sam nor Molly wasn't an inviting prospect.

Blue lay down again. "I'm going to have a rest, then go to Value Village."

"It's just up the hill." Sam waved his hand. "An easy walk."

"Nice." Blue closed his eyes and waited for Molly's Skype call.

***

"What?" Molly leaned so close to the computer Blue was afraid she'd bang her head on it.

"A fire. Everybody in the building is out, no one knows for how long, but I expect months at least. Sorry, I didn't even think to grab anything from your room."

"Nothing there I can't stand to lose." Molly shook her head. "I can't get my mind around it."

"I'm still in shock." Blue leaned back. "Sam is off to Toronto tomorrow; his son is paying the airfare. After we've talked, I'm off to Value Village for a few new clothes.

"I never knew someone who lived out of one drawer like you."

"Old habits." Blue shrugged.

"Make sure you take care of yourself. I'll be back by the end of June. I've already contacted the University about their Social Work degree."

"That's great." Blue grinned and his heart lifted. "I'm proud of you."

"Grandma's going to write me a reference." Molly frowned. "I'll worry about you."

"You're allowed, but only for an hour on alternate Wednesdays. Put it in your calendar."

"Yes, sir." Molly saluted and stuck out her tongue. "I have to go. I've got early shift tomorrow."

"I'm still waiting for a picture of you in your uniform."

"You're going to be waiting a long time. Tim Horton's is a nice place to work, but the uniform does nothing for me." Molly laughed, blew him a kiss, then disconnected.

Sam had already gone to bed to be ready for an early flight in the morning. Blue stripped down and crawled under the covers. The motel room already felt emptier. He'd gone from a loner to a person who needed people. He supposed it was healthy, but he didn't look forward to trying to find his balance yet again.

Value Village would have delighted Molly, but Blue bought what fit and got out.

***

When he woke in the morning, Sam had gone. Blue rolled out of bed and scrubbed his face with his hands. The fire was like a nightmare, would he end up on the street again?

There were people all around him in the same boat, displaced from their lives, uncertain of the future. Self-pity was a waste of energy.

Chapter 2

Wednesday, May 11

People he recognized from the apartments stood outside their doors in the fresh air, talking in groups. A couple looked up to stare at him but no one waved or spoke.

Blue took the sturdiest chair from his room and sat outside. The sun warmed him. He called Al to let him know what had happened and that he'd be a few days before he returned to work. The battery flashed yellow. Blue turned the phone off and put it in his pocket. He'd need to get a charger soon.

A man with dark black skin walked past with a big dog on a leash. Glossy black with a massive head, it turned to gaze at him for a moment before the pair hit the sidewalk and headed up the hill.

"That's a mean one." A man stood beside him, a beer in one hand.

"Big and black doesn't make a dog mean." Blue looked up at the man, "I can get another chair if you want to sit down."

"Wasn't talking about the dog." The man leaned against the window. Blue got up, pushed his chair over, and fetched another one from the room.

"Name's Sasha." The man planted himself on the chair and took a long pull from the beer.

"Blue."

"That guy lived across the hall from me. Never heard

Columbia Smoke

nothing from his mouth that wasn't a complaint."

The scent of the beer called to him.

"Some are like that." Blue forced himself to stay relaxed, but his gut tightened despite his efforts.

"True." Sasha finished his beer and stood up. "Time for a refill — you want one?"

"No thanks."

"Just as well — I only got two left." Sasha laughed and went into the room next to Blue's and came out with a fresh beer. He sat down and grunted. "Work gave me the day off — want me in tomorrow. At least most of my tools are locked in the truck. Had to buy boots though." He pointed at his feet, "Hate breaking in new boots."

"What trade?" Blue looked at his own ratty shoes.

"Electrician. You?"

"I work with the Peer Ambassadors."

"Heard about them. Street people, right?"

"Partially. We all have the lived experience of homelessness but not all have slept cold."

"Spent a year in a trailer so I'm not one to judge." Sasha stared at the can in his hand as if surprised it was there. "You need electrical work, call me. Don't worry — don't drink on the job."

"Long time back, I used to say that." Blue closed his eyes and hoped Sasha didn't ask the logical next question, but he finished his beer and walked away. Blue sighed in relief.

A woman with a young face and old eyes walked across the parking lot to him. "Can I bum a smoke? Get it back to you on payday."

9

"Sorry, don't smoke." Blue smiled. "Name's Blue." She walked away without replying and he shrugged.

"Careful talking with her." Another woman sat down beside him, reeking of tobacco smoke but at least without a cigarette in her hand. "She started the fire by heating up drugs in her apartment."

"Really?" Blue raised his eyebrow. "You work with the Fire Commissioner's office?"

"What?" The woman frowned at him. "Well, screw you." She jumped up and stomped away.

Doing great Blue; you're one for three. He shifted to get more comfortable. He had no injuries from the fire, but for some reason, couldn't sit still.

Women pushed carts of laundry to a room on the bottom level of one part of the 'L' shaped building. Other people drove in and out in nice cars. *"Not all the guests are from the fire".*

"Wonder why we have to cross the street to eat when there's a restaurant here?" a young man paced back and forth in front of Blue.

"Contracts; business; who knows?" Blue gave up following the young man with his eyes — it was making him dizzy.

"Guess." The young man didn't slow his pacing.

"My name's Blue."

"Simon. You think we'll be able to get into our place today? All my game stuff is there."

"I doubt it will be today, but I expect we'll hear from the property management company soon."

"Shit!" Simon banged his hand on his leg.

"You know where I can get a charging cord for my phone or laptop?"

"Dollar store in the plaza across the road from Value Village will have phone cords. Computer place in the mall might have something for your laptop." Simon stood still and stared up at the cement overhang, "Why do you have your laptop?"

"Grabbed it as I walked past — forgot to take the power cord."

"Should have brought my game system." Simon walked down to the end of the row of rooms and went into the last one, four doors down from Blue.

The man with the black dog returned. Again, he kept his eyes front, but the dog assessed Blue as they passed. They climbed to the second floor of the new building.

"You from the fire?" A young woman in a suit carrying a clipboard stopped in front of Blue.

"Name's Blue. 312."

"There's a meeting in half an hour in the room below the restaurant." She pointed to the far end of the motel. Go 'round the back, not through the restaurant."

"Thanks." Blue nodded at her as she checked something off on the clipboard.

***

Blue walked into the meeting room filled with people showing varying degrees of discontent.

Simon wasn't the only one wondering when they'd get into their rooms, and Valerie, the representative from the property company, had no definite answers.

"Sorry, until the Fire Commissioner's office clears it,

we can't allow anyone in. There are people watching the building twenty-four/seven, so your possessions are safe from theft."

She asked about tenants' insurance but only three out the forty or so residents had any. Blue hadn't bothered. He didn't own enough to worry about it, but he'd get some for the next place. One of those with insurance was the guy with the black dog. Other people in the room glared at him.

"My company will work with you if you wish to look for a new apartment," Valerie gave a twisted smile, "We won't hold you to the lease. Any who want their damage deposit back should be able to pick it up at the office next week."

Blue headed back to his room. He had time to kill before lunch. At the office, he asked if he could rearrange the room.

The man behind the counter looked up. "As long as you don't break anything you can do what you want. You from the fire?"

"Yup."

"You'll get housekeeping once a week."

"Fine with me, thanks."

Blue returned to his room and spent some time heaving one of the beds up to lean against the wall, giving him more space to put the table and chairs.

After the room was in shape he walked across the street for lunch.

His voucher didn't cover everything on the menu. He had a choice of three entrees or soup and salad unless he wanted to pay extra. Blue picked a beef sandwich with fries, telling himself he'd get the salad the next day. The servers gave him as much attention as he needed, even with him needing to show his voucher at each meal.

Eating restaurant food constantly gonna get old quickly. Blue walked up to the SaveOn and picked up some snacks and a package of coffee. He went to Value Village to buy a coffee maker and while he was there, a tiny crockpot to go along with the coffee maker and a frying pan, and he found a jacket. It wasn't leather but it would help keep him warm. His purchases set on the counter in the tiny kitchen, but Bill sighed and went back out to get fresh air.

A group of people at the end of his row of rooms were gathered and yelling at someone Blue couldn't see.

He walked over and saw they'd backed the woman with the old eyes against the wall of the new building.

"Chill!" Blue slid past the group and turned to face them.

"She started the fire." It was the woman from before, who'd blamed the fire on the one they were yelling at.

"Whatever! Yelling at her isn't going to fix anything," Blue jerked his thumb at the office where the man stood in the door looking at them. "But it could get you tossed from here for being a nuisance."

The woman looked like she wanted to argue but the others were already moving away.

"They hate me." The woman with the old eyes sounded like she half agreed with them. "I fell asleep with something on the stove."

"It is going to be tough living with that but don't let them paint you as the cause of all their problems."

"Why do you care?" she looked halfway to tears.

"I wouldn't like to be the kind of person who didn't care." Blue waved his hand, "Defusing fights is sort of what I do at work."

"My name's Tara." She turned away. "Don't get mixed up with me — I'm cursed."

Blue went back to his room. The woman who had led the charge to blame Tara swore at him as he passed. He ignored her and took his seat by the door. One of his chairs had been moved over to Sasha's door — no big deal.

The afternoon reminded him of the days trying to fill the time between waking and sleeping when he'd lived on the street. The smallest things became fascinating. The man with the dog had the end room on the second floor of the newer building. The dog lay by the railing and surveyed the parking lot.

The angry woman's name was Wanda. She had lived above Tara and her apartment had been one of the ones filled with flame. She was another person with insurance. Though it didn't stop her endless litany of complaints. He could hear her from her room at the far end of the old building.

Fran stayed in the same room as Simon and her stack of rabbit cages. She was asked for money to pay for animal food.

"Call the SPCA," Blue suggested, "I expect they'll help."

"They won't take my rabbits away?" Fran wrung her hands.

"Why would they?" Blue pointed at the cages. "You're

obviously taking good care of them."

She walked into the room where Simon sat staring blankly at the TV.

"Need to borrow your phone."

He handed it over and she immersed herself in typing. Blue left her to it and went for a walk around the buildings.

"Just can't stop interfering," Wanda sneered at him as he walked by her. "Asshole!" She grabbed his arm, "I'm talking to you."

"I have no interest in listening." Blue pulled his arm loose. "You're only hurting yourself. I couldn't care less about what you think of me." He breathed away the spike of anger in his gut.

"I can make a lot of trouble for you," Wanda's eyes narrowed.

"Probably." Blue went back into his room and closed the door. With nothing better to do, he turned on the TV. The five o'clock news had just started. They had an interview with someone from the building. Blue didn't recognize the man.

"It is tough for all of us. I'm fortunate to have insurance but most of the residents don't, so they are particularly hard hit. I'd like to ask the community to do something to help them."

They played a clip of the fire raging before the firetrucks arrived. The news anchor announced that residents in at least one apartment, hadn't made it out. That would make Tara feel even worse. The Fire Commissioner had no comment.

After covering the wildfires across B.C. they moved on

to the apparently never ending question of a performing arts centre in the downtown.

Blue took his evening meal to go from the restaurant across the road and walked up the hill. He'd heard a couple of other people talk about the view from a park by the Panorama Motel. The view was worth the effort. All of downtown Kamloops and the North Shore stretched between him and the mountains. He sat at a picnic bench and ate.

The big black dog bounded over and jumped up on him. Blue fed her the last bite of his hamburger.

"You're a beauty, aren't you?" Blue scratched her ears.

The dog's owner strode up to him. "Please don't feed her without permission." He frowned at Blue. He was slight and moved like a coiled spring, like he was ready to attack at the slightest cause.

Blue tensed, then chastised himself. The man was no more likely to be dangerous than Blue, just because he had dark skin. "My apologies." He thought both of feeding the dog, and his assumptions. Blue wiped his hands on the napkin and gathered up the garbage from his meal.

"Come, Harley." The man snapped his fingers, and the dog took position at his heel like he'd pulled on a leash. The pair walked away. The man bent with a bag on his hand to pick up something and then tossed it in the trash can. Blue stuffed his trash in too, then went back to admire the view a bit more before heading up to look for charging cords. He couldn't find anything for the laptop but found a cheap charger for his phone.

Tomorrow he'd look up the bus routes and get down the hill to work.

Chapter 3

Thursday, May 12

The bus grumbled its way up Columbia. Blue admired the sunlit view as he watched for his stop. He was pleasantly tired from a day of walking on Tranquille and around the river, cleaning up needles, and helping people — sometimes just being someone who'd stop and talk. It wasn't that long ago he'd been all but invisible; he knew how it felt.

He got off the bus and walked down to the motel. Harley had her nose through the railing watching the goings on below. Blue waved at her then walked over to his room. The chair by his door was gone and he didn't see it by any of the doors on his level. The woman in the office simply nodded and made a note when Blue reported it.

Instead of bringing out another chair, Blue dropped his bag in his room and then headed up to the Superstore to see if they had camp chairs in. While he was there, he picked up some granola and milk for breakfasts. He wouldn't have time to eat at the restaurant before work on the early shifts. Blue walked back to his room with his oversized camp chair and bag of groceries.

He put his food away, then set up the chair and parked himself.

Wanda had a group of people around her; all with the same disgruntled frown on their faces. They looked suspiciously at Blue. She stomped over to him. The reek

Columbia Smoke

of stale cigarettes enveloped him.

"Did they charge for the chair?"

"Chair?" Blue looked up at her.

"Don't play dumb with me. You left your chair out last night, now it's gone and those —"

"If you're planning on a racist rant about the people running the motel or some of the other guests, I'm not interested." Blue met her eyes, "Whether they charge me or not is none of your business."

"Some of us don't trust them," Wanda frowned, hands on her hips.

"Tough!" Blue waved his hand. "That's your problem, not mine. I'm sure you're welcome to find another place to live."

"The Emergency Services won't pay for a different motel."

"Then either you stay here and be grateful, or move on. Either way, leave me out of it."

Wanda huffed and stalked away to talk loudly to her coterie, waving her hands at Blue. The group all had a similar look; hard eyes, frown lines — they were probably talking about how White people were discriminated against. He'd met some like them on the street and learned to avoid them.

After supper the manager came over to Blue. He was an average looking guy, unless you hated people who weren't white.

"Sorry sir, but someone has complained that you are being in the way sitting out here."

"Do I look any more in the way than anyone else?"

Blue pointed down the strip of rooms with chairs and coolers, even a table outside.

"No, but I must be seen to respond to complaints." The manager frowned, "Some of these people…" he let the sentence drop. "Sorry to have bothered you."

"You aren't bothering me." Blue smiled at him, "You're doing your job. I have no problem with that."

"Thank you." The manager walked back to the office.

Sasha came out his door holding a beer and sat in his chair with a sigh.

"They bugging you too?"

"Depends on who you mean by 'they'." Blue shook his head.

Sasha drank from his beer can and stared out at the parking lot. "Stuff like this fire. — it shows what's really inside us. I don't like it."

"Can't change other people." Blue pulled his legs out of the way to let Simon pass.

"Yeah."

"By the way, put the chair in your room at night. Seems someone is taking stuff."

"Too much of a bother — let them have it."

"It's from my room." Blue stretched his legs out. "If I put in my room, it's not coming back out."

"Right." Sasha stood up and carried the chair into his room, closing the door with a bang.

"Doing great today."

Sam would have had some words of wisdom for him; probably tell him if it wasn't his circus, they weren't his monkeys. Blue fetched his phone and turned it on. There was a text from Molly asking if he was doing okay. He responded that he'd gone back to work and had a good day. She didn't need to worry about the bickering residents. Blue sent a message to Sam asking how he was handling Toronto, then put the phone in his jacket pocket.

Supper was yet another burger this one with a salad. Blue returned to his room and put the chair outside again. Staying in the room reminded him too much of how alone he was. When evening came the air chilled and Blue was about ready to go in and get ready for sleep — maybe a chat with Molly first.

Shouting from the other end of the new building made him stiffen and old reflexes almost sent him out of the chair. Blue settled back. 'Not his monkeys.' They were loud, probably drunk, but didn't seem to be beating on each other.

A few minutes later a police car pulled in and parked by the office. The cop went into the office for a minute then came out and went upstairs. The shouting match had cut off as soon as the car turned in, but the professional tones of the police officer suggested he was a warning the people involved.

Blue picked up his chair and carried it inside. He ate an apple while he booted the computer and checked the battery. Thirty percent, he'd save it for later. Instead, he texted Molly again and they chatted about her day for a bit before he showered and went to bed.

***

Screaming outside had him sitting bolt upright in bed. He peered out the window, but the noise had stopped and nothing moved where he could see it. It took some time before he could relax enough to get back to sleep.

Blue dreamed about the fire, only Molly was in the apartment and he couldn't get to her. He woke up and smelled smoke. Checking his room showed no source for the smell and he couldn't smell it outside when he opened the door. Someone ran across the parking lot and disappeared into the stairwell on the new building.

Must have been an after effect of the dream. The smoke odour had gone completely. Blue lay down again but his eyes wouldn't close. He pulled out his phone and searched for apartments until he grew tired enough to sleep.

***

Living in the motel was a new kind of tedious. Wanda expanded her complaints to cover Harley's owner. Somehow having insurance was reason enough to gain her dislike. It didn't matter that she'd made the choice not to buy it. He took his supper to the overlook to get away.

Blue saw Harley's owner at the Panorama. Harley bounded over.

"Sorry, girl — need your boss's permission."

"Harley, sit!" The man came over and rubbed her ears and she grinned. "What's your name?"

"I'm Blue."

"Harley this is Blue. He's okay, you hear me?"

Harley barked once and Blue held his hand out for the dog to sniff. She licked his hand.

"If necessary, she'll do what you ask."

"I'm honoured," Blue scratched her ears.

"You must be special. Haven't seen her take to

someone like that in a while."

"Always liked dogs. Didn't think it fair to make one live on the street with me."

"You don't live on the street now."

"Still adjusting to that." Blue stretched and lifted the last bit of his burger. The man nodded.

"Catch, Harley." Blue tossed it and she snapped it out of the air.

"I'm Rod," the man said. He crossed his arms over his chest like introducing himself made him nervous. "Abira was a friend of Harley's. He died in the fire; his cat and his wife too."

"That has to be tough, losing a friend like that."

"Harley is still a bit down, but she'll be better now she has a friend." Rod snapped his fingers and walked away. Harley gave Blue a last sloppy grin and ran after her master.

After that, Blue made a habit of eating his supper at the outlook and saving a bite for Harley. Rod never said much more than "Harley, sit", but after a day walking Tranquille with the Peer Ambassadors, Blue didn't mind the quiet.

Chapter 4

Friday, May 20

Meeting at 6. V.

Blue pulled the note off the door and checked the time on his phone. He had enough time for a shower if he didn't mind eating after the meeting.

Valerie leaned against the table at the front of the room.

"I'll make this quick so you don't go hungry. The Fire Commissioner has cleared most of the apartments for tenants to retrieve important items. You will have half an hour and will have to wear a mask and sign a waiver. The fridges have been taped shut. Leave them for the clean up company. "

Simon raised his hand. "When can we go?"

"I have a list. You can sign up for a slot now, starting tomorrow at ten. Don't be late or you won't get in."

Blue signed up for a slot in the mid-afternoon on Monday. He could leave work early.

***

Blue stepped off the bus and walked around to where a van was parked. A woman with a clipboard was talking to Rod, who signed the page and put on a disposable mask. Someone in a tyvek suit and full face mask led him into the building.

"You're Blue?" The woman flipped a page on her clipboard. "This is a waiver. The smoke is toxic, but it should be no problem if you stay less than half an hour."

"Just need a few computer cords; maybe a few dishes."

"My advice is to stick to glass or metal — plastic may absorb the smoke — same with paper and cloth. Unless it is irreplaceable, leave it." She handed the clipboard to Blue.

"We already got the irreplaceable things out." He scratched his signature and gave the board back.

The tyvek suit returned and Blue put a mask on. They trudged up the stairs to the third floor. The carpet was black and the walls might have been painted in shades of grey and black by an abstract artist. Blue wrinkled his nose; the stench of the smoke already making his throat dry.

They unlocked the door.

"Half an hour then sign out. I don't want to have to check if you're dead in your apartment."

"Shouldn't be more than a few minutes."

He took a good frying pan and a pot from the kitchen — put cutlery and a few cooking utensils in the pot. The apartment wasn't as marked by soot as the hall, but it still stank. Blue fetched his computer cables and then grabbed the scarf Molly gave him at Christmas. It was in a closet in a box; it would be fine.

Sam had said he didn't need anything, and Blue would have no idea what was important. He pushed the door to Molly's room open and walked in. The room was as sparsely decorated as the rest of the apartment. She'd only lived in it for a few months before going east. A sketchbook lay on the desk and a tumbler held pencils.

There were only a few blank pages in the journal — most of it was doodles, but Molly had tried portraits of

25

him and Sam. Blue took the book and the two other full ones in the drawer of the desk.

Blue initialed the list on the way out to show he'd left the building. Rod stood at the bus stop; a suitcase and a bulging bag beside him.

"Get everything you need?"

"My record book is gone," Rod frowned. "They must have taken it."

"Record book?" Blue pulled out his bus pass as the vehicle lumbered to a stop. Rod struggled to lift the suitcase and the bag. Blue took the suitcase and grunted. It had to be filled with rocks.

Rod sat across the aisle clutching his bag and not saying anything. Blue was getting used to the man's silence. They changed busses at the Landsdowne exchange and rode up the hill to the motel.

At the bottom of the stairs to the upper floor, Blue hefted the suitcase up to Rod's door. Harley greeted him with a tail wag and a grin. Rod scratched her ears, then unlocked his door and dragged the suitcase in, then his bag. He nodded at Blue and closed the door.

Blue scratched the dog's head, "I'll see you at the outlook," and then headed to his room. He left the journals to air out on the table and plugged his computer in to charge. The dishes went into the sink to wash later.

The prospect of cooking didn't appeal to him but if he went to get supper now, he'd be waiting a long time for Rod and Harley. *"Waiting never hurt me yet."*

***

At the lookout, a crowd lined the guardrail. They buzzed

with conversation.

"Batchelor's on fire." A young woman looked caught between shock and excitement. She pointed across the river.

"Been a dry spring." An old gent leaning on a cane shook his head, "Heard they evacuated a few houses."

At first all Blue could see was the smoke, then he saw the line of red traveling slowly across the grass. He took his supper over to the picnic bench and sat with his back to the view. Watching someone's home in danger of fire didn't appeal to him.

The man with the cane sat across from Blue.

"Already it's a bad fire season and it's not even started yet. Someday the flames will consume everything. All we'll pass to our children will be the smell of ashes." He didn't look like he expected an answer so Blue unpacked his supper and ate while it was hot. The older man wandered away.

Rod walked over, Harley staying beside him like she was glued to his leg.

"Heard Batchelor's burning." Rod sat and Harley plumped down beside him.

"That's what I'm told." Blue wiped his fingers and tossed Harley her bite. "Think I've had enough fire."

"Came here five years back after a fire burned through my place and a dozen others. Insurance wouldn't pay so I'm stuck here. Place has good blueberries."

"Better blueberries than ashes."

Rod tapped his fingers on the table. "Don't like that they took my record book."

"What would anyone want with your record book?"

Rod stared at Blue and absently petted Harley.

"Every repair request I know about in the last three years. People want the silliest things."

"What kind of things?"

Rod looked away toward the smoke rising behind Blue. "You think I'm strange."

"I lived on the street for years —" Blue swivelled to look at the crowd still ogling the fire. "I've no right to think anyone is strange."

Rod stood and snapped his fingers. Harley grinned at Blue then followed her master.

After a while, Blue tossed his garbage in the can and followed Rod. The crowd didn't look to be thinning.

Blue talked to Molly but she was writing more exams and he didn't want to distract her too much. He lay on his bed and stared at the ceiling. He'd never once considered the condition of the building they lived in. The lights went on and off; the water came out of the tap. It was better than the street.

He needed to do better; if not for him, for Molly. She'd be going to a university in the Fall, and he wanted a stable home for her.

Without transition, he woke in the dark to shouts and sirens. For a moment he was back sleeping in the brush by the river, then reality came into focus.

Lights flashed through the curtains and Blue got up to look. An ambulance parked, lights off, while the three squad cars turned the parking lot alternately blue and red.

He didn't want to join the rubberneckers in the night,

but he couldn't sleep or concentrate on anything else. Finally, he booted the laptop and requested a video call to Molly's computer.

"Hello." Molly tugged her blanket tighter around her shoulders. "What's wrong?"

"Flashing lights and an ambulance outside." Blue's hands shook.

"Look at me." Molly leaned in closer to the computer, "Breathe and keep your eyes on me." She talked to him until the trembling stopped.

"I'm sorry to have woken you," Blue sighed and rubbed his eyes. At some point the lights had stopped without him noticing.

"Don't be silly!" Molly shook a finger at him. "We're family."

"We are." The last bit of tension in his chest softened.

"You going to be okay?" She looked worried.

"You're coming home the end of June, right?" Blue grinned crookedly. "...only a few weeks. When you get here, we'll go apartment hunting. I'm thinking of trying to find something up here near the university. The bus runs often enough to the north shore."

"That might be nice, but I'll miss being close to the river."

"Wait until you see the view. I'll send you some shots."

"That'd be nice," Molly yawned. "You going to be okay?"

"I am," Blue sighed. "Thank you."

"No probl—" The connection cut off and Blue staggered back to bed and slept. His dreams all had smoke leaking in from the edges.

Chapter 5

Saturday, May 21

Blue walked out the door to be greeted by Wanda's 'I-told-you-so' face.

"That druggie OD'd last night. Good thing she didn't burn the motel down. At least we're safe now.

"Aren't you in a good mood." Blue glared at her, restraining his anger. "Celebrating someone's death. No one, no matter how broken, should be mocked in death. Now get out of my way."

Blue stomped away to the sound of Wanda's screamed curses. The volume made up for the lack of imagination.

He walked up to the outlook. The crowd was gone, as was the fire on Batchelor. Hopefully, the only thing to burn was grass. As if thinking summoned it, the smell of burning made him cough.

Damn! I hate fire season. Blue scanned the landscape dimmed by smoke from fires burning all through BC.

Maybe it was a side effect of being off the street, but the smoke bothered him more now — more time to worry about things that he can't change.

"Heard the woman screaming at you." Harley licked Blue's hand as Rod stepped up beside him at the rail, "Good job."

"Don't know about that, but gloating over a death is not the way to make my day."

Rod's laugh was rocks grinding.

"Wherever I go, there are people who care more about their drama than being human. They're like vultures on a kill.

"I know the feeling." Blue ran his fingers down Harley's back, "Can't let the vultures eat you."

"Don't understand addiction but I see it consume people." Rod stared out at the haze, "Being in the world is hard but no one gave us a choice." He snapped his fingers and Harley followed him away.

Blue stood lost in thought, vaguely aware that other people came by with and without dogs. He got Rod's bitterness but that was a void he'd stay away from. Molly helped him see that he had little choice about the life he was given but had a lot of choice over how he lived it.

His stomach growled and Blue laughed. Breakfast sounded like a better idea than philosophy.

After the plate of bacon and eggs, Blue went for a walk to explore the area. All he'd seen was Value Village and FreshCo.

There were a lot of opportunities to spend money in the area. Winners was an education. Even at deep discounts, most of what was there cost more than he'd ever spent on clothes. The kitchen section bewildered him.

Blue found a waxed canvas coat very different from his usual leather. It fit and was the first jacket he'd seen that did. Molly would tease him about it — something to look forward to. On the way to the till, he picked up a package of dog treats at half-price.

Blue strolled back to the motel, still coming to terms with the new jacket.

"Manager would like to talk to you," one of the service staff pointed at the office.

"Thanks." Blue headed over and waited as a customer complained.

"I am not used to being woken by such vile language." The man signed his bill, "I won't be back."

"Sorry you had to hear that, sir. We have spoken with the person in question and if there are any more such outbursts she will need to find other accommodation."

"I'm surprised you let someone like her in here in the first place."

"We have a contract with Emergency Services, and everyone deserves a place to live."

The customer sniffed, wheeled his immaculate luggage out to his BMW. Then took off with a squeal of tires up Columbia, leaving the screech of tires, honking horns and middle fingers in his wake.

"There are people who make it a compliment to have them angry with you," Blue sighed. "What did you need to see me for?"

"That woman told me you came out of your room and pushed her out of the way."

"Right!" Blue rolled his eyes.

"One of our staff saw the incident and told me there was no pushing but the woman only ranted more because the staff person is Filipino. I wish I could tell her to leave but the contract insists they get two chances."

"I like the way you think," Blue shook his head. "It isn't easy to be fair like that."

"Thank you, sir. Sorry for the trouble."

"Not your fault," Blue smiled. The smile dropped from his face as he pushed through the doors. He'd met plenty of racists on the street, as if being White made them special. To attack someone only because they looked different was beyond his understanding.

Wanda stood outside her door to sneer and wave a middle finger at him. Blue smiled broadly and waved back, then laughed as her face reddened in anger.

He booted up the computer and started looking at what was available in two-bedroom apartments. The prices made him wince. The money in the bank was to help Molly become what she wanted, not to pay for a swanky apartment. The search was the new jacket, only multiplied. Life wasn't a daily struggle on the edge of a precipice now, but he'd moved only a step or two away.

His phone rang. A young man from the property management company wanted to know if Blue intended to take a cheque for the damage deposit.

"Sure, do you have any apartments available?" Blue described what he was looking for.

"Not up in that area. Try the Kelson Group. They are good and have a lot of places around the city."

"I will take the cheque then, thanks." Blue rubbed his forehead.

"It will be ready for pickup at the office in three days."

"Great! You've been a big help." Blue hung up the phone and sighed. They found the place that burnt because Molly had that social worker helping her look. Blue didn't relish finding the next one, but he hoped to have a few choices by the time she got home.

"Home?" Blue looked around. He'd slept in worse — much worse. It would do for now.

***

"Hello." Wanda answered her phone

"You're attracting attention." The voice made her skin crawl.

"You told me to be myself. This is me."

"The others are not as stupid as you. Stop it!"

Wanda opened her mouth to argue but instead disconnected the call and threw her phone on the bed.

Chapter 6

Tuesday, May 30

Blue went into the Tim Horton's on Tranquille for a break from the smoke in the air.

Constable Madoc stood in line for coffee. When it was her turn, he stepped in front of her and told the girl serving the coffee that it was on him.

Madoc muttered something into her mic as she led the way to a table in a corner and slid into a chair. "Let's sit for a bit and get caught up. Thanks for the coffee."

"Not as much sugar as your usual," Blue smiled.

She laughed. "What have you been up to?"

"You know Molly's off at school? She's going to the university for social work in the fall. If I had a calendar, I'd be marking off the days."

"What happened to your calendar?"

"It's at the apartment which is unlivable because of the fire in the building."

"I heard about that — didn't connect it with where you were living. Did you lose much?"

"Nothing important," Blue shrugged and sipped at his coffee. "I'm still not used to owning things."

"That's better than not being able to let things go."

"I know people like that. They're a reason I'm reluctant to get comfortable with being comfortable."

"Not sure if I should envy you or not. Having minimal bills to pay each month has to be nice." She played with her cup, "Where are you staying now? ...not back on the street I hope."

"Emergency Services is putting us up in a motel at the top of Columbia."

"Glad to hear that," Madoc leaned back.

"You still with Car 40?" Blue waved at his partner, Travis, on the street. "There was an overdose death at the motel and this woman was gloating about it."

"Gloating isn't illegal."

"True, but I can't imagine being that mean without needing help. Her place burned worse than mine. Maybe if you did some follow up on the OD and happen to talk to her…"

"I will see what I can do but no promises." Madoc stood, "Thanks again for the coffee — next one's on me." She headed for the door. Blue used the washroom then took his turn outside talking to the young people while his partner had a break.

"You some kinda wannabe cop?" The man was probably ten years younger than the forty he looked.

"Nope, we're peer ambassadors. I've been where you are, so if you need to resolve something I may be able to help."

"Nobody wants to help." The man swayed dangerously, "Jus' more people to control my mind." He tapped his head hard enough to make Blue wince.

"Hey man! Got any water?" A younger woman Blue saw around Timmies a lot, came up to him, "Need to wash my hand off."

Blood poured from split skin over her knuckles.

Blue pulled a bottle of water out of his pack and then dug out the first aid kit.

"What's that for?"

"Putting a bandage on so your hand doesn't get infected."

"Don't need no bandage."

"Hard to punch someone with no hand." Blue started to put the kit away.

"Okay, just this once." She held out her hand and Blue wrapped gauze on it, then held it on with tape. Red already oozed through the bandage.

"If it doesn't stop bleeding, or if it turns nasty, go to the hospital and get it taken care of."

"Sure, sure!" She wandered away admiring the bloody bandage.

"Uh, can I get water?" The man still swayed but didn't look as aggressive.

"Of course!" Blue gave him a bottle of water and a card. "Call this number and if we can, we'll find you."

"If you can?" He peered at the card doubtfully.

"You want immediate help, call 911."

"As if!" He staggered away, bumped into a car, setting the alarm off, and kept going. Someone came out of Timmy's to yell at him.

"Can't you stop those people?" The man buffed the car with his sleeve.

"Stop them from what?" Blue stepped back, "...from living? ...from being part of our society?"

"People like you are part of the problem — wanting to give everything to people who don't deserve it. I worked hard for my money."

"I'm sure it was very taxing to make sure you were born white, male, and in a well-off family."

The man threw a punch like he knew what he was doing. Only he was too far back for it to do more than knock the dust off Blue's vest.

A siren hooted and the man spun around with a mix of guilt and fear on his face.

A squad car pulled into the parking lot. A big cop climbed out and swaggered over.

"I was told there was a fight going on here."

"The one you're thinking of is over and done," Blue pointed toward the alley. "If you see a woman with a bandaged hand, she might know something about it."

"What is going on between you two?"

"A philosophical discussion — I won." Blue kept a carefully straight face, "No harm done."

"What's with the blue vest? PAN?" The cop peered at Blue.

"The Peer Ambassador Network. We help resolve problems before the police or bylaws need to intervene."

"Right! I've seen your type before. Stay out of the way of real cops." He stomped back to his cruiser and drove away ignoring the annoyed glares of people he'd blocked in.

Blue sighed and shook his head, "Must be new in town, haven't seen his face before."

"You know all the cops?" The man looked at Blue with uncertainty.

"Most of the ones on the North Shore." Blue

shrugged, "It comes with the territory."

"Sorry I got a bit carried away." The man looked sheepish.

"No harm; no foul." Blue waved it off, "I'm a bit on edge myself." He handed a card to the man, "This will explain a bit more of what we are about."

The man took it cautiously and Blue left him staring at it.

"What's up? You're normally the cool one." Travis sipped at his coffee.

"Maybe the fire is bothering me more than I want to admit."

"Yeah, that has to suck." Travis stuck his notepad in his pocket. "I got the number of the cop car."

"Maybe post it on the board as someone to be extra careful around." Blue hoisted his pack, "We should get back to it."

***

Thankfully, the rest of the day was comparatively quiet. Blue rode the bus up to the motel. He'd met cops like the one at Timmies before; people who made being a cop a lifestyle more than a job. Even as a cop, he'd made a point of keeping his distance. That was a long time ago in a different life.

A shower helped relax tension he hadn't realized he was carrying. He dried off feeling more up to fetching supper and seeing Harley and Rod.

The big dog took away the last of the jangled nerves.

"Rough day?" Rod wasn't looking at Blue but at Harley.

"Much better now," Blue chuckled. "I have to thank you for the privilege of meeting Harley."

"I don't do people well." Rod scratched Harley's ears. "I have a mask I put on, but it doesn't fit well."

"I think I get that." Blue stretched. He dug a treat from the pocket of his coat to give to Harley. She snapped it up.

"Don't need a mask for Harley." Rod patted her.

Blue tossed her another treat, "I'm not big on masks either."

Rod almost looked at him.

Harley licked Rod's hand and he walked off with the dog trotting at his side.

Chapter 7

Monday, June 5

Blue dropped his bag on his bed and headed straight to the shower. He let the sweat and exhaustion wash down the drain.

Working as a peer ambassador was rewarding but demanding. He let go of a store owner's ire at a person he saw panhandling everyday, and who had no interest in being anything more than what she was. Letting go of the desire to fix people was one of the hardest parts of the job.

When the burdens of the day were gone, he climbed out and dried off, and put fresh clothes on. He didn't feel like eating yet, so he parked his chair outside the door and enjoyed the smoky sunshine. Days of smoke acclimated him to the smell, only on really bad days did his throat bother him.

"Haven't seen you 'round much," Simon danced from one foot to the other.

"You get your game system?"

"Yeah, but the wifi here is too slow makes the games glitchy."

"That's rough." Blue put a sympathetic face on, "How are Fran's rabbits?"

"Fine, I guess. She went back to her mom's with them. Can't blame her."

"Sounds lonely." Blue glanced up at the young man.

"I guess. Her mom doesn't like me. Says I should get a job instead of playing games all the time. Jobs are boring."

"Are your games never boring?"

"Grinding levels can be a drag but you have to do it to get to the next level." Simon paused in his shifting and stared at Blue. "You think a job is like grinding levels?"

He wandered off without waiting for a reply.

"Meth-head!" Sasha sat with a beer in his hand and another under his chair. "His girlfriend paid for the drugs — he's got to be jonesing bad."

"Perhaps," Blue said. "We all have our problems."

"I'm fine. I work all day and drink all night." Sasha winked at Blue and opened his second beer. "...only way I can stand this shitty life."

"Been there." Blue looked up to watch Rod and Harley heading up to the outlook.

"Right! And now you gotta fix everyone else." Sasha crushed his beer can then stomped into his room and closed the door.

"Can't fix people," Blue said to the empty chair, "...never sticks."

Melancholy pulled at him. He wasn't sure where it came from, but it sucked at his energy. Since the fire, he'd been short tempered — speaking without consideration. Blue pulled out his phone and dialed a number.

He got an answering service.

"Hey, Sam! I could use some of your special non-advice. Give me a call when you have a chance."

Molly wasn't at the computer but probably working.

Gloom attacked him, making him consider banging on Sasha's door until he handed over one of his beers.

Blue sat and stared at nothing until Harley loped over and Harley tried to climb into Blue's lap. "Harley missed you," Rod said.

Blue buried his face in Harley's fur and held on, trying to breathe instead of falling apart.

The bleakness rolled over him, but the warm weight of the dog anchored him in the world and pushed back the tide of loneliness.

"Thanks, girl." Blue whispered when he could find his voice. She licked his face in response, then padded over to lie down at Rod's feet.

"I get days like that." Rod crouched down to rub Harley's side, "Sucks."

He stood and walked away. Harley looked at Blue as if to ask if he would be all right, then followed her master.

***

Blue slept without dreams but woke up tired, expecting fire alarms. The fire in the apartment made him hypersensitive to the smell of smoke.

He took the bus down the hill and struggled through his shift with PAN.

"Something's wrong," Travis handed Blue a coffee. "...your head isn't in it. Don't get me wrong, I'm not dissing you, but you're going to get hurt at this rate."

"I think the fire is getting to me." Blue slumped into a chair in the PAN office and put his coffee aside, "I thought since I had nothing to lose, it wouldn't bother me to lose anything."

Travis sat and moved Blue's coffee back within reach.

"Why did you think you had nothing to lose? You had a home and now you're in a motel: you had a friend but he's across the country."

"I guess you're right." Blue thought about drinking the coffee Travis poured but it looked too heavy to lift. Gravity had doubled suddenly, and he couldn't move. He needed Harley but she was up on Columbia. The heaviness grew until it became too much work to keep his head up.

"Blue." The voice was familiar but the name wouldn't come to him. A hand landed on his shoulder "...you don't have to be strong. Let your friends help you."

A shudder ran through Blue making him feel both weaker and lighter.

"I guess I'm not so good at being alone anymore," He sighed and lifted his head. Constable Madoc sat on the corner of the table and his eyes widened.

"Travis thought to give me a call. You got good friends here."

"I do." Blue looked around The Big Edition office, shared with PAN. Travis leaned against the door to the main room. Dabra, administrator and layout person for The Big Edition, sat at her desk, but facing him.

"You need some proper food." Jake put a bowl of soup in front of Blue and a roast beef sandwich beside it. Blue tucked in and with each bite the darkness lessened.

"Thank you." Blue shook his head ruefully, "I'm glad to have so many friends smarter than me."

"The view from the inside is different." John sat at the end of the table. "We all need help to keep life straight."

45

"Right!" Blue took a deep breath. "I think I should pay a visit to Interior Services and get someone to talk to properly."

Travis put his phone in front of Blue. He picked it up and hit the speed dial they all had on their phones.

"Hi. My name's Blue. I'd like to make an appointment for intake."

***

"I hope you don't mind sharing Harley with me." Blue played with the dog's ears as she drooled on his knee.

"You know where I live." Rod perched on the picnic table, looking at the view instead of Blue.

"Thanks." Blue slipped Harley a treat from the pocket in his jacket. There was a hole in the pocket. Somehow that made Blue happier with the coat. Pieces of dog treat floated between the canvas and the lining.

"You're the first person, aside from Harley, who's never asked what's wrong with me."

"Nothing's wrong with you..." Blue threw a dog treat at Rod's back, "...different isn't wrong."

"Not according to the other nine billion people on this planet," Rod snapped his fingers and Blue was left alone with a large slobbery spot on his jeans.

After staring at the view for a few minutes, Blue headed to the motel. The computer was beeping as he entered. He ran over to hit the accept call and Molly's worried face filled the screen.

"I saw that I missed your call last night and I've worried all day."

"I hit a rough spot." Blue sat and tilted the screen to

see better, "Last time I felt that bad, I walked away from my life. Good thing I have good friends. Not to mention Harley."

"I want to meet this dog you keep talking about." Molly tried to smile and failed. "Are you all right?"

"No," Blue sighed and leaned back, "but I'm getting the help I need. Sorry to worry you."

"I'm coming home," Molly frowned then jumped up to pace in her room.

"Will that affect going to university in the fall?"

"My grades are all in but for one exam."

Blue didn't say anything, though he had to bite his cheek to stop the words.

"You aren't going to tell me to stay and finish?"

"No. I'm sure your grandmother will do enough of that!" He laughed and rubbed his eyes. "To tell you the truth, if you could climb through the computer, I'd be the happiest man in Kamloops, but it is your decision; not mine, not your grandmother's, and I know you will make the right one."

Molly's eyes filled with tears. "I will give notice at work and ask the teacher if I can write the exam early." She leaned in close to the computer, "You call me every day. You miss a call; I'm on the next bus."

"Deal!" Blue smiled and put his finger on the screen where the tears rolled down Molly's cheek.

Chapter 8

Tuesday, June 6

Blue swallowed the last bit of coffee, then waved at the waitress. She had blue hair, tattoos, a nose ring, and a warm smile for everyone who entered the restaurant. He walked out to the bus stop, hoping he never lost the appreciation of having eaten a good meal

***

The bus rumbled down the hill. Blue had first thought about walking, but he didn't want to be tired for his appointment.

Years ago, he'd seen a counsellor at the suggestion of his superior. It never clicked and after three sessions Blue had canceled his next appointment and turned to the bottle.

If he'd kept going, would he still be a cop?

It didn't matter now. He would have to have lived a different life — been a different person. More to the point, Blue liked his life now.

The bus stopped at the exchange and Blue strolled along Landsdowne to a familiar building he'd never entered.

"I'm Blue."

The woman behind the counter looked at her list and smiled at him.

"Have a seat and someone will be out to fetch you in a few minutes."

He looked around the room; comfortable chairs, brochures and old magazines on the table, a heavy door and thick glass separating the woman's office from the room. Other people sat not looking at each other. A man looked carved from stone, and a woman bounced her foot and fussed with her hair.

"Blue?" a man who didn't look much older than Molly opened the heavy door.

"That'd be me." He stood and followed the man through the door and down a hall lined with wooden doors. The man opened one and waved Blue in.

"Have a seat." The man sat and picked up a clipboard. "My name is Amhoud. We'll start with a few questions."

Over the next half hour, they ran through his history; the red room, the drinking, Molly, and the fire.

Amhoud was surprisingly easy to talk to and Blue spoke of things he'd never considered sharing.

"Thank you." Amhoud set the clipboard aside. "The interview can feel very intrusive, but you've worked hard and made my job easier. The next step is to talk about what kind of help you want. I can refer you to a psychiatrist, but you'll have to wait awhile for an appointment. We can also meet a few times. I'm a registered counsellor, not a doctor, so I can't prescribe anything, but talk itself can be powerful."

"I think seeing a psychiatrist would be a good idea, but I want to do something right away, too." Blue shifted in the chair, "Last time I felt like this, I lost a career and years of my life."

Amhoud leaned back, "Tell me more about that."

Blue left the office with an appointment in two days and an oddly light step.

He walked over the bridge to the North Shore, more ready to work than he had felt since the fire.

Amhoud had warned Blue that his emotions might become more volatile. At the LOOP, Blue had a bowl of soup and waited for Travis.

"How'd it go?" Travis sat beside him.

"I think it went well. I have another appointment for Thursday. If I get strange, give me a smack."

"I think I can do that," Travis grinned.

The rest of the day went well but walking from the bus stop to the motel, Blue's feet dragged. He showered, taking longer than he needed to wash the tiredness from his soul.

Rod was standing at the rail when Blue arrived.

"When do you eat? I've never seen you at the restaurant."

"I cook for myself." Rod didn't turn his head, "I'm insured so I don't get meals and the rest."

"Never thought of that." Harley bumped Blue's hand. "Sorry girl — shouldn't be neglecting you."

"She has taken a shine to you."

"It's the treats." Blue tossed one to her.

"Harley's more than just a dog," Rod said. "She reads people's hearts. If anything happens to me, she'll be your dog."

"I'd rather have both of you, but I will take care of her, if necessary."

"Good." Rod pointed across the river, "There's a fire

on the reserve side but we can't see the really bad ones. That's life — the really bad stuff we don't know about until it is too late."

"I know what you mean," Blue looked over at the pillar of smoke, "but I wonder if the same is true of the good things."

"Maybe." Rod left. Harley gave Blue's hand a final lick before following him.

***

Blue woke sweating and gasping, an undefinable terror gripped him. He couldn't move even to turn his eyes. At the outside edge of his peripheral vision, red and blue flashing lights lit up the curtain and he was free. Blue jumped up to turn on the room light. He was alone. The cruiser was parked in front of the manager's office. Blue recognized the number on the car and his gut curdled. Any thought of going to see what was happening vanished.

Instead, Blue took a shower — as much to wash away the fear as the sweat. When he finally climbed out, he wrapped himself in a towel and fell into bed.

In the morning, he might as well have run a marathon. He shuffled like an old man to get dressed. His legs ached even after he'd had breakfast and packed for his day.

The bus took him down the hill, and he began to feel better — as if the sun through the window warmed more than his skin.

At the LOOP he went into the office to pick up the reports from the last shift. Not much was the way he liked it. Some complained when it was boring but Blue couldn't shake the idea that boring was safe; if not for him, then for others.

The afternoon went quickly. He and Travis were headed toward the LOOP when Blue spotted a police car in front of the Redbeard. "Let's check it out."

Travis rolled his eyes as he crossed the street.

The manager and a police officer were talking to a woman who flailed her arms dramatically. Blue recognized the officer as one he'd seen before on Tranquille.

"Good! Maybe you guys can get through to her." The manager stepped back so Blue could talk to the women.

"I'm no thief. I pay for what I get."

The cop looked at Blue. "Apparently she used a coupon for a free coffee. She heard one of the staff say it was out of date but that she didn't want to turn the woman away. Peggy insisted on paying for the coffee but didn't have enough money, so she tried to get them to take cans from her cart." The police officer crouched down to talk to the woman, "Look these guys are here to help you."

"I pay for what I get." The woman glared at Blue and repeated, "I'm no thief."

"No one is suggesting you are." Blue pulled a chair over so he could talk more comfortably. "They're just worried about you."

"Phaah! Don't need to worry about Peggy — anyone knows that."

"What do you think the solution is?"

"They can take my bag of cans — it's worth more than the coffee — but say they can't because of some health regulations. Whoever heard of a regulation against empties?"

"They don't seem to have a lot of space for your cans." Blue looked around, "How about we loan you the money and you pay us back after you cash in your cans?"

"What's to stop you from running off? I pay my debts."

Blue opened his mouth to respond but the world tilted suddenly and he clutched at the chair to keep from falling.

"Hey! You okay?" Peggy leaned toward Blue.

"Just a little dizzy from the sun." Blue put his hand on his head.

"Tell you what I can do," Travis stepped forward, "I'll walk with you to General Grants and you can pay me as soon as you get your money."

"That'd be fine. Just don't be trying to introduce me to Jesus or nothing."

"Promise."

"You want some water?" Peggy put a hand on Blue's shoulder, "I got a bottle in here somewhere."

"Thanks Peggy, but I'll get a glass for him." The manager put out his hand. "I'm sorry for the misunderstanding."

"You're righteous." Peggy shook his hand, then headed north pushing her cart. Travis looked at Blue and raised an eyebrow. Blue nodded, so Travis caught up to Peggy and said something to set her cackling.

The manager put a glass in Blue's hand. Blue drank the water. It sent coolness down his throat and he imagined the change on a heat camera as he moved from orange to yellow to green.

"Good to see you in action." The police officer stood

and stretched, then took out his notebook to jot down a few details. "You going to be alright?"

"Probably." Blue didn't try to stand yet.

The officer nodded and went to his cruiser, then drove off after a few moments of talking on the radio.

"Do you need a ride somewhere?" The manager filled up Blue's glass again.

"Don't want to put you out." Blue rubbed over his eye where it felt like a nail was trying to push its way out of his skull.

"Nonsense! I can leave for a few minutes and the gang can run the place."

"Maybe if you run me up to my motel...I think if I lie down a bit I'll be fine."

***

The insistent beeping of the computer dragged Blue from his doze and he sat down to hit the accept button before Molly panicked.

"Hi Blue!" His mom smiled at him. "Molly's friends dragged her out for a goodbye evening. I promised to check in on you."

"Thanks." Blue rubbed at his head where the pain was returning. "Did she fill you in?"

"She did. I was prepared to loan her my car —would be faster than the bus. She's a good driver."

"Hadn't told me she'd done her driver's test."

"It's part of the program. Gets the women ID and independence in one shot."

Blue closed his eyes, unable to use his ears and his eyes at the same time. Then described what he was feeling to his mom.

"Sounds like the trauma is working its way out. You might want to go check it out at emerg anyway."

"There's something else I'm going to try first," Blue sighed and rubbed his hands on his legs. 'If that doesn't help, I'll go. I'll call you."

"Be sure you do, or I might have to come along with Molly. "

"It would be good to see you." Blue pushed the heel of his hand into his left eye. "I'm going to go and see a friend." Blue stood and let the world settle down before heading outside.

Harley lay on the walk outside Rod's door. She woofed; the first noise he'd heard her make. Blue took it as encouragement and pulled himself up the stairs and flopped down beside Harley, back to the railing. She licked his face, then put her head in his lap and didn't look like she planned to move.

As he rubbed her fur and listened to her breathing, pieces of himself reassembled, though he wasn't completely sure they were in the right order. Leaning his head back against the railing, Blue sighed and closed his eyes. The disorientation and pain receded.

"Wanna a Coke?" someone asked. Blue lifted his hand and a cool can was placed in it. He opened his eyes to see Rod crouched in front of him. When Blue took a sip from the red can, Rod sat against the wall facing him and drank his own Coke.

"Heard Harley, but figured you'd need some time before I butted in." Rod finished his can in one long swallow, then carefully put it aside.

"Felt like someone shook up my puzzle box, then dumped it out on the floor.

"Used to like puzzles." Rod tilted his head, "Wouldn't be fun to be one."

Blue let the silence grow. Like Harley, it was healing, and he had no need to break it.

Blue wasn't sure how he got back to his room. His memory insisted that Harley carried him. His brain scoffed. He fumbled at the computer and got it to call Molly's.

She answered, then leaned back, a hand over her heart.

"Grandmother told me about your conversation and I've been sitting here waiting for your call."

"I'm mostly back together," Blue said. "There's this dog named Harley. I'm beginning to think she's magic."

"I can't wait to meet her."

"I expect you'll get a chance," Blue smiled. The odd sensation told him it was the first of the day.

They talked until he started nodding off and Molly told him to get to bed.

Chapter 9

Thursday, June 10

The fear woke him in the night again but a warm presence against his back formed a bulwark against it.

"Good dog." Blue closed his eyes and returned to sleep.

In the morning, he found that one of the pillows was jammed up against his back. It didn't matter; the thought that Harley was there had been enough to carry him through the night.

He headed down for his appointment at Interior Services, picking up a coffee and a bagel to eat as he walked along Landsdowne.

The process went the same as last time with more focus on the present issue than the past leading up to it.

"Believe it or not, your reaction could be seen as a good sign," Amhoud tapped his pen on the clipboard. "Put it this way — a short talk created a lot of movement. The last two days were the result of your mind trying to integrate your new understanding with your present life."

"What about the dog? I've never experienced anything like it."

"Perhaps your mind has fixed on this dog as a point of stability. The way you describe relaxing when you are in contact with her suggests a powerful connection. It certainly isn't doing you any harm."

"So I will randomly come to pieces? I can't work if I

might fall apart at any moment."

"You may want to consider taking some time off until things settle a bit."

"And how long will that be?"

"Could be a week; could be a month," Amhoud shrugged apologetically, "though I'm hoping if you remain this focused, it will be closer to the week."

"Work is the only thing keeping me sane." Blue sagged back in his chair, "I don't know what will happen if I sit around with nothing to do."

"I expect you to work on your mental health the same as if it is a full-time job. Think of it as an investment. You will come out the other side of this more integrated and self-aware."

"Great!" Blue closed his eyes and took a deep breath, "I will meet with you twice a week?"

"That will be important...and I will give you a number to call if you feel it is an emergency."

"Emergency?"

"You will know. I'd rather you call if you don't need to, than the other way around."

Blue called Dabra and told her he'd be off work for at least a week and maybe longer.

"Take care of yourself," she said.

"That's the plan." He walked up the hill toward the motel. The piece of paper in his pocket suggested some things he could try: keeping a journal, a sketchbook, and walking. Amhoud had written in, "*Spend time with Harley,*" and underlined it.

Blue's gut ached and his hands trembled in his pocket.

His legs were tired, but it distracted him from the anxiety. The dollar store would have notebooks he could use. It reminded him of the first time he'd bought drawing materials and Molly had claimed them.

He picked up a journal which would be large enough to draw in but small enough to carry with him. Pencils, erasers, and a case to hold them, joined the book in the basket. They had light packs with string instead of straps. He wouldn't want to carry any real weight in it, but the book and the pencil case fit inside.

While he was in the area, he went to SaveOn and bought more elaborate groceries than he'd been living on. Cooking would kill time and he could impress Molly when she arrived.

As much as he didn't like her leaving school early, his heart lifted with the thought of seeing her again. His mom wouldn't let Molly do anything to risk her future.

The bags pulled on his arms enough to distract him from the strings on the pack. He'd have to make them longer somehow.

Harley wasn't watching through the railing, so Blue put the groceries away and headed up to the outlook to find her and Rod.

Wanda stood beside a cop talking to Rod. From the look on Rod's face, it wasn't a friendly chat. Wanda turned to look at Blue with a sneer on her face.

"What's the problem, Officer?" Blue used his Peer Ambassador voice.

The cop glanced around to see Blue. "Oh great — it's you." It was the new cop he'd run into at Tim's.

"Rod and Harley are friends of mine." Blue put a smile on his face.

"Really? How convenient." The cop didn't take his eyes from Rod.

"We live in the same motel." Blue kept the smile, though he wanted to snarl. "Same as Wanda here. The apartment building we all lived in burned."

"You know her?" The cop's words carried a frown. "She said this man's dog threatened to bite her."

"Harley?" Blue laughed. "Come here girl." Harley bounded over to lick Blue's hand. He rubbed her head. "She wouldn't hurt a fly unless it threatened her master."

Blue kept his eyes on Harley. She'd come over eagerly enough, but her chest vibrated with a silent growl.

"You can always ask the manager about Wanda. I don't think there is a person in the motel who she hasn't complained about."

"Keep that dog on a leash." The cop stomped off to his cruiser. Wanda had vanished while Blue watched the cop.

"Put a leash on Harley?" Rod's hands clenched.

"He just needed to have the last word." Blue stretched his hand out to put on Rod's shoulder but Harley bumped in between them, pushing Blue back. "Okay, girl. I get the message."

"That bitch threatened me." Rod ground the words out, "She needs a leash more than Harley."

"Agreed," Blue stepped back further, "but anything you try to do will only give her more power. What I would do is buy a cheap leash at the dollar store and hook it to your belt. It won't humiliate Harley but it will be enough to satisfy most police officers."

"I hate the cops." Rod spoke in his usual flat tone but Blue heard the venom in the words.

"I can understand that." Blue watched as the cruiser pulled out and turned away from the motel. "I wonder if some of them like being hated."

He looked back at Rod only to find that he and Harley had also disappeared.

***

After he'd eaten supper (a pork chop with BBQ sauce and a salad), he sat at the table and pulled out the sketchbook. He tried to draw Harley and her goofy grin, but it came out looking like a snarl.

To be truthful it looked like a snarling cow. Blue laughed and closed the book. It would be a while before he'd be close to what he could do years ago before his life went off the rails. Even then he hadn't been as good as Molly.

The important thing wasn't the quality of the picture but the emotion.

What would make him draw a snarling cow?

The computer beeped and he accepted the call.

"How was your day?" Molly leaned both elbows on the table.

"The counsellor suggested I take some time off work. So...I'm supposed to be writing in my journal and sketching..." He held up the picture.

Molly hooted with laughter and fell back on the floor.

"Maybe we should hang it on the fridge when you get

home."

Molly's laughter turned into howling which brought her roommate over, which turned into another gale of laughter.

"Whooo!" Molly gasped, "I needed that." She wiped her face and returned to look into the computer.

"Glad to help," Blue smiled at her. "How was your day?"

"Wrote my last exam." Molly's smiled faded. "I promised the boss to work to the end of the two week schedule — that's Sunday. I didn't expect that leaving would be so hard."

"If it were easy, it wouldn't mean anything." Blue rubbed his eyes with the heel of his hands. "I mean, I miss you like crazy because you're important to me."

"That makes sense, but it doesn't make it any easier. We're having a graduation party in June, but I won't be there."

"The busses run both ways, Molly. Wait and see."

"You're right. It's just…" she got up to pace, "I'm worried about you and I'm already missing my friends. I don't know where I want to be — except I do. We'll all go our separate ways anyway and I have to be there for you."

"I'm selfish," Blue sighed. "Making you rush home."

"It was my idea, and after the dreams…"

"Dreams?" Blue asked when she didn't continue.

"A vicious monster hunting you. I try to get to you to help but you and it disappears before I can get there."

"We'll defeat it together." Blue put his hand on the screen and tried to rub her tears away with his thumb.

Chapter 10

Friday, June 11

A card was taped to his door. It read: *'Kelly Pashes, Insurance Adjuster'*. He turned it over. *"At Starbucks until 4 pm. I'll buy coffee."*

Since he had nothing else to do for the moment, free coffee sounded good. Wandering up the hill, Blue tried to think why an insurance adjuster would want to talk to him.

At the Starbucks, a person in a suit sat taking notes on a clipboard with one of the other tenants. A nameplate identified the person as Kelly Pashe.

"You waiting for Kelly?" A young man in jeans and a polo shirt looked at Blue with a raised eyebrow.

"I am," Blue smiled at him. "I'm Blue, from Apartment 312."

"Great! Go ahead and order a coffee; whatever you want." He handed Blue a slip of paper. "There are a few people ahead of you."

"Thanks." Blue went to stand in line. He ordered a large black and was handed it immediately. The note made a lot more sense if they were meeting everyone. No matter; he had more free time than he wanted.

Watching Kelly talk to the tenants kept him from getting bored. Some sat down and started talking before Kelly could. Others shifted uncomfortably, visibly staring at Kelly. They was dressed deliberately androgynously — it was the only way Blue could put it. Conservative suit; pink blouse but with a power tie; man's watch on the wrist, and dangling earrings. He smiled. If people were occupied with trying to figure out Kelly's gender, they'd not be thinking about what they were saying.

"Blue.!" the young man stood beside him.

"Thanks." Blue carried his coffee over and sat across from Kelly. Androgynous or not, they were very attractive.

"Should thank you for the coffee." Blue hoisted it and took a sip. "Can't remember the last time I had fancy stuff like this."

"The least I can do for making you wait." Kelly's voice floated between contralto and tenor.

Blue smiled. "No problem." He took another sip and waited, not paying any more attention to Kelly than he would anyone else.

"I like you," Kelly said. "You don't buy the most expensive coffee on the menu because I'm paying for it and now you're sitting here like I'm just one more person."

"Aren't you?" Blue leaned forward a bit, "a person? That's all I need to know."

"Thank you…" they looked at the pad of paper, "Blue."

"What can I help you with?" Blue leaned back again.

"Let's start with your experience of the fire."

Blue told them about waking up; the smoke; grabbing his computer but not the cords; the door that stuck, and being glad that Molly was safe in Alberta.

"Your roommate, Sam, is he still in town?"

"Gone to his son's in Toronto. I will ask him if it's all right to give you his number."

They smiled, "How conscientious of you!"

"We value privacy." Blue met their gaze and Kelly laughed.

"Is there anything else you can tell me about the fire?"

"A woman, Tara, was blamed for it. Don't know if it's true. She died of an overdose a few days after the fire."

"Sorry to hear that. Did you know her well?"

"Only to see her. Her eyes looked a hundred years old."

"You don't think she could have caused the fire?"

"Anyone could have caused it. Word is she left something on the stove and went to sleep."

"Good thing the smoke alarm woke her in time to get out."

"Don't know. Ours didn't work that well. It went off when we had a shower but didn't when I burned dinner to the point we had to open the windows to get rid of the smoke. Honestly, I think the thing went off that night, but the place was pretty cloudy with smoke. Outside there was a jet of flame coming out her back wall. The building was an *I* shape. She had a place on the end, looking west."

"I see." Kelly made some notes, then gave Blue a wide smile. "Would you like to join Tom and me for dinner? It is rare to find someone comfortable enough with me that I can relax."

"I would be delighted." Blue wrote his phone number down. "Just let me know where you're eating. I don't have a car, so if it isn't too far from here, I'd appreciate it."

"One of us will call. I'll get Tom to find a place — he's good at that."

Blue shook their hand and carried the last of his coffee outside. He had the rest of the day to kill — might as well pick up his sketching materials. Maybe he'd end up with something other than a snarling cow.

Sitting on the guardrail wasn't ideal but Blue worked on sketching the view. He tried to figure out which had been his building, but it was trickier than he'd expected.

"Excuse me!" A younger version of Tara, or she might have been older but with younger eyes, stood beside him, "I'm looking for the hotel where my sister had been living."

"You looking for Tara's place?"

"Tara?" The woman's eyes went wide, "You knew her?"

"We lived in the same building. I saw her at the motel a few times before…" Blue let the sentence die as tears welled up in the woman's eyes. "Why don't you take a seat." Blue patted the rail beside him, "I'm Blue."

"Nessa." The woman sat and dried her eyes with a tissue. "What was she like the last time you saw her?"

"Sad." Blue closed his sketchbook and put it away. "Some of the other tenants had her cornered. I sent them away but Tara told me she was cursed."

"She mentioned you…" Nessa stared north at the

rivers, "...said you protected her. She couldn't understand it."

"Everything is rumour and speculation until the Fire Commissioner makes a report. Doesn't matter if the fire started in her place, stuff happens. I've burned my share of suppers."

"She was an addict. I've lost count of the number of times I talked her into rehab. Tried to get her to come live with me but she needed the action of the city, the drugs and the rest." Nessa gave a choked laugh, "She had no concept of personal safety — told me she had the balcony door unlocked so her boyfriend could visit without coming through the front doors."

Blue waited while she fought for control.

"I'd like to see the room where she died." Nessa wiped her face, "Maybe that's morbid."

"Come on. I'll introduce you to the Manager. He's a reasonable person."

The Manager wasn't in and a woman who might have been his daughter worked the desk.

"I don't know." She looked up the record. "It isn't rented at the moment, but it's been cleaned and made ready. If you go in, I'll have to get housekeeping to go through it again."

"How about if I rent it for the night?" Blue pulled out his wallet to fish for his debit card.

"Are you sure?" Nessa looked like she wanted to run.

"It's the best way — you'll have as long as you want. I'm not paying rent so I can afford it." Blue signed the paper and got the key. "Did housekeeping save anything from the room — personal effects or something?"

"I'll check."

Blue led Nessa over to Tara's room; a carbon copy of his except no mini-kitchen. Sterile. Impersonal. It could have been any motel room in any city.

Yet, Nessa walked around touching things as if they held cherished memories, then sat on the bed and sobbed. Blue put the key on the table and left her to her grief.

He sat outside his room and wondered if he'd died on the streets, would his family have grieved the same way? Probably.

Nessa came out of the room and Blue walked over to meet her.

"Did you get what you needed?"

"I think so." Nessa handed Blue the key, "She was younger than me. The last one to leave home. I never knew her as well as I should have."

They walked into the office as the woman finished with a customer.

"Sorry. Your sister didn't have much, but they did find this." She slid a cookbook across the counter: *"The Low Fat Diet"*.

"Oh my God!" Nessa picked it up and opened it. "...I gave her this. The doctor said she had gall bladder problems."

As she thumbed through the book, Blue could see comments on the recipes. *"Tastes like crap"*; *"Tastes like shit"*; until one page the scribble read, *"Not bad! Nessa'd like it"*.

Nessa held the book to her chest like it was a treasure.

"Thank you so much, both of you." She fled the office

with tears running down her cheeks.

"You have your debit card?" The woman wiped at her eyes, "I'll process a refund — the boss will understand."

Blue wandered back to his room. As he settled into his chair, his phone rang.

"Where's a good place to meet you?" Tom asked.

"That Starbucks will work. It is only a few steps from the motel."

"Can you make it for five? We'll give you a ride."

"Sure!" Blue glanced at the time. He'd have a shower before he left.

***

Kelly parked the car by The Noble Pig on Victoria. Blue had worried his jeans and t-shirt would be too casual but Kelly had changed from the suit into leggings and oversized blouse.

Kelly ordered Intergalactic Pretzels and a Big Bad Wolf beer. Tom asked for a Stone House.

"Sorry, alcohol and I went through a messy divorce a few years back." Blue pointed, "This Cast Iron thing looks good."

He sipped at his water. Not that long ago, he would have been shaking with the desire to share the beer. That went nowhere good. Let them enjoy it.

The insurance company had flown in Kelly and Tom from Edmonton. They were specialists in more complicated and high value claims.

"They aren't happy that at renewal three months back, the client increased the value of the property. We would have been sent anyway — fires are tricky. The tenants who died — their family is suggesting they would have survived if she hadn't fallen on the parking lot in the winter. She was using a walker and her husband would have stayed with her regardless of his own safety. We found what was left of the walker yesterday."

Their meals came and they dug in, Kelly telling stories of other cases they'd been involved with, some of them comic and a few tragic.

"The Fire Commissioner's office will be releasing the report tomorrow. The cause was a grease fire in the kitchen of the unit next to the victim's.

"Grease fire?" Blue frowned.

"What's wrong?" Kelly put their glass down and fixed on him with their gaze.

"I spent part of the afternoon with Tara's sister. The only thing Tara took out of her apartment was a cookbook about a low fat diet. Nessa said Tara had gall bladder trouble."

"So, you're wondering why she'd be heating oil at two in the morning?" Kelly sighed, "People are unpredictable. Maybe someone had come over and she was cooking for them."

"Nessa did say that Tara left the balcony door unlocked so her boyfriend could visit without her needing to buzz him in."

"There you go." Kelly went back to eating but they looked distracted.

After supper, Kelly and Tom dropped Blue off at the motel.

"Thanks for joining us, sorry for talking shop."

"We always talk shop," Tom rolled his eyes dramatically.

"My pleasure." Blue waved and went into his room and called Molly.

"How are you doing?"

"I hate packing," Molly scowled. "Even if I leave most of the stuff behind, there's still too much to bring on the bus."

"Why don't you just bring what you need?" Blue leaned forward, "Your grandmother won't mind, and we can arrange to get it later."

"I guess." Molly looked around at her room. "It isn't like I'll have much space until we get a new apartment. I've been looking online and it's expensive up that way."

"We'll figure out something," Blue shrugged his shoulders. "I spent some time drawing something other than vicious cows." He showed her the landscape.

"How come you didn't finish it?"

"A woman came by — sister of the one who died of the overdose and is supposed to have started the fire. I ended up having supper with two insurance adjustors."

"Women?" Molly wiggled her eyebrows suggestively.

"Well, no." Blue tried to find words to describe Kelly, "They didn't fit the usual categories, but were interesting. I enjoyed supper."

"I'm glad to hear that."

***

"What?" the man paced in the small room.

"This guy who's getting chummy with that weird broad — get rid of him. Don't want her staying any longer than it takes to sign the release."

"Not smart — someone will get suspicious."

"Bah, don't know what I pay you for."

"You pay me because I'm smarter than you."

"Don't push it. I'll take care of it my way, but your take is getting thinner."

"Do what you want."

Chapter 11

Saturday, June 12

Blue dragged himself out of bed. Yesterday, he'd had Kelly to entertain him. Now that they'd returned to Edmonton, he was on his own.

Harley greeted him with her usual enthusiasm at the outlook but Rod scowled down at the rivers, barely visible through the rain.

"What's up?" Blue gave Harley a treat as he stepped up beside Rod, then sat on the rail.

"Work stuff. Nobody's ever happy."

"Don't think you've mentioned work before. What do you do?"

"I'm an adjustor." Rod stalked off. Harley looked at Blue with puzzled eyes.

"Better go with him, girl." He patted her flank as she took off to catch up with Rod.

Blue's cell buzzed as he ambled back toward the motel.

"Hello."

"Blue, it's Kelly. You have time to talk?"

"Time is one thing I'm not short of these days."

"I'll be by to pick you up in five."

He'd hardly got to his room, before their car pulled up. Blue chucked the chair inside and locked the door.

"Not much security to those doors." Kelly started off as soon as Blue's seatbelt clicked.

"I talked to the investigator to get more details than

were in the report. The fire started at the stove, then spread to the whole kitchen all at once. She figures someone tried to put it out by throwing water on it."

"Tara didn't have any burns even with it starting in her place." Blue rubbed his forehead, "People blamed her for starting the fire, and I think she blamed herself, but she couldn't remember it."

"Her statement to the fire investigator was that something woke her up and the apartment was already on fire. If she'd left grease on the stove on high, that would make sense." Kelly banged the steering wheel, "Add water and it doesn't work. I can't imagine someone getting away with no burns at all. Grease fire and water's the next best thing to an explosion."

"I don't think I like where this is leading," Blue sighed and looked out at the houses; a mix of old and new.

"Sorry, I can take you back." Kelly made a quick u-turn that had Blue holding on tight.

"No, I'm in it now — nowhere to go but through."

"Tom's meeting with a building inspector today. He's wondering if there's something the owner would rather not deal with."

"Have you talked with the owner?"

"I haven't even been able to find out who they are. They're buried behind shell companies. The management company is handling it for now but if it gets dicey, they'll drop it."

"So why me?" Blue glanced over at Kelly — their imperturbable shell was badly cracked.

"I need someone to bounce crazy ideas off of. Tom's

not bad at it but I have a hunch you're better."

"Bounce away then and we'll see."

"If the fire was deliberate, somebody had to set it. I can see Tara accidentally setting the place on fire but not planning it."

"What about that boyfriend Nessa talked about?"

"I have to look into that." Kelly drove out of Kamloops. Blue wasn't sure where they were going but he pushed it out of his mind.

"You need to consider method." He stared at the rockface they were passing. "Figuring out how it was done will get you halfway to who did it."

"Any ideas?" Kelly roared past a line of slow campers struggling uphill. "I specialize in large claims, not fires specifically. A convincing enough theory will get the bosses to hire an expert."

"Nobody we know of was burned. The police could check with the hospital to see if someone came in with severe burns."

"I called and the person said they'd get back to me."

"So, assume for the moment no burned person is running around Kamloops. I can't see anyone putting themselves at that much risk."

"How would they set the fire then?"

"A device of some kind. Something beside the pot which would tip water in when the grease lit up."

"Anything like that the investigator would have caught it. All he found was a big pot on the stove."

"If you lived alone, how big a pot would you have?"

"I have a two-gallon pot I use for stock and corn."

"So we say a two gallon pot is reasonable. How much oil would you need to cook a few fries?"

"Not much. When I fry wonton balls, I put in just enough for them to float."

"Right. Your big pot wouldn't be your first choice for fries."

"Hell no! Not unless you're doing a whole chicken and you'd need a death wish for that."

"Good — big pot, lots of oil. We're getting somewhere."

"Why lots of oil?"

The rain grew heavier and now traffic was sparse. They'd turned off the main highway?

"Why use a big pot if you aren't going to fill it?" Blue kept his eyes on the clouds.

"They needed a lot of oil to make sure the fire spread quickly." Kelly nodded sharply and had to break at a sudden curve

"Now we need the system they used to send flaming oil all over the place."

"Anything mechanical, the investigator would have found. There was just the pot and nothing else near it."

"Damn! That isn't enough." Kelly slammed the wheel again and Blue winced.

"Leave it for a while." Blue made juggling motions with his hands, "Let the subconscious work on it while we talk about something else."

"Like what?" their knuckles were white on the wheel.

"You like cooking. What's your favourite dish to prepare?"

"Cooking?" Kelly shook their head, "I make a wicked Moroccan chicken spicy enough to make you warm all the way through, but not harsh. It's about grinding the spices only enough…"

Blue tried to keep up with them but they jumped from Morocco to Thailand and away to Mexico. At least talking about food was calming Kelly but Blue's stomach wanted some of it.

"Granola bar?" Blue pulled two out of his pocket.

"You always carry granola bars in your pocket?"

"Most of the time. Dog treats too, but I expect the granola bars taste better."

"Hey, these are high class!"

"Don't like to eat stuff that tastes like crispy squares. A little shop had these at a good price so I bought a box."

"Nice!"

They reached a town with a big ski hill. Kelly turned around. "I thought a drive in the mountains would be relaxing," Kelly snorted. "Should have known better, can't relax with this fire eating at me.."

"No harm." Blue peered through the rain. No vehicles on the other side — they must be getting close to home.

Then the road disappeared from beneath them. Kelly fought to keep the car from rolling as it careened down hill. They hit something which locked their seatbelts, then something that activated the airbags.

***

Blue groaned. Airbags hit more like a hammer than a marshmallow.

The driver's seat was empty and the door was open. Blue's

door wouldn't budge so he crawled across the seats to clamber out of the car. Kelly stood twenty feet away. They looked like they were screaming but Blue heard nothing.

"Hey, take it easy!" They were beating their head with clenched fists. Blue grabbed one arm.

"Don't touch me!" Kelly spun around to backhand Blue's face, sending him stumbling back...white spots obscuring his vision.

"Oh God!" Kelly collapsed to their knees on the wet ground, "I'm sorry. I just..."

"Don't worry about it. You were in full panic mode. It was worth a slap to have you calm again."

"This is all my fault." Kelly shivered and looked up the slope. The road was barely visible above them.

"Don't think I could get up that slope. One slip and I'd be done for." Blue said.

"I'm sorry," Kelly looked miserable.

"Get in the car and pop the trunk. I'll see if there is any kind of emergency kit."

He found a tiny red bag and carried it back to the front seat to explore its contents.

Kelly's lips were blue and their teeth were chattering.

"We have to get you warmed up. Crawl into the back seat." He pulled a tiny packet of silver film from the red bag and handed it back to them. "Emergency blanket. Wrap it around you and get out of your wet clothes. It doesn't need to be winter to die of hypothermia, you need to take care of yourself."

"Blue..." Kelly whispered a few minutes later, "...the banket is so thin — I still feel naked."

He took off his jacket, pulled his t-shirt off and passed it back to them, then put his jacket back on. The kit had a candle and matches. With the front door not completely closed, they'd be safe from carbon monoxide.

It was scary how much colder he felt without the t-shirt. The last granola bar poked at his side.

"Here — get some energy into you."

"What are you going to eat?" Kelly asked. Their teeth had stopped chattering.

"I still have a pocket full of dog treats," Blue laughed.

"How can you laugh at a time like this?"

"I spent years on the street, sleeping cold until I got sober and smartened up...moved into the apartment last summer...wasn't in it a year. The street taught me to hold things lightly and value people more. Laughter is a survival skill."

He nibbled on the dog treats. Harley would forgive him. They tasted like bland beef jerky — not bad at all.

Kelly stayed silent so long that he worried they'd gone to sleep. He glanced back — their eyes were black holes in their face and silent tears smeared makeup on their cheeks.

"You okay?" Blue asked. "Sorry, but I don't think it's a good idea for us to sleep, in case of concussion.

"Come in the back seat with me," Kelly whispered. "If we share our body heat, we both will be warmer."

Blue scrambled back and Kelly held the blanket open. When he'd sat, they crawled into his lap, still shivering. Blue unzipped his coat and wrapped it as far around them as he could. They relaxed against him and he wrapped his arms around them to keep the blanket closed.

"Blue, I haven't been held since…" Kelly shuddered, "…I didn't like to be touched. Shaking hands was as much I could manage. But this is…" They turned to face Blue and kissed him on the lips, "…it's nice." They put their arms around Blue's neck and buried their face in his shoulder.

The candle burned out and it began to get dark. The rain had let up and the occasional rumble of a passing truck filtered down to them. Blue shuffled around to reach forward and turn on the emergency flashers — might be dark enough for someone to notice. He leaned his head back and listened to Kelly's even breathing. They were right — it was nice.

Chapter 12

Sunday, June 13

Knocking woke Blue, for a moment, he thought he was back on the street trying to protect Molly. His arms tightened, then he saw the firefighter's face.

"Any injuries?" she yelled through the glass when he got his eyes to focus on her.

"Nothing physical."

She radioed up the hill and soon two stretchers were lowered followed by two more firefighters.

"Kelly?" Blue shook them gently and prepared himself for a panicked reaction.

"Mmmmph," Kelly looked at him and kissed him again.

"The rescue is here," Blue said.

Kelly stiffened and gasped as if they couldn't decide whether to fight their way out or cling tighter.

"You're okay..." Blue used the same voice he did when someone on the street was out of control, "...I've got you — you're safe."

"I have to get dressed!" Kelly's voice rose toward panic.

"Your clothes may still be damp — just the pants and you keep my t-shirt on."

Kelly squirmed around until they sighed, "That's as good as it's going to get."

The firefighters wrenched the door open and Blue

passed Kelly to them. They visibly fought for calm as the woman coaxed them onto the stretcher. Kelly flailed their arms when the firefighter tried to do up the straps.

"Wait a minute!" Blue crawled out of the car and over to the stretcher, "You can do this — it's only until you're safe." He leaned down and kissed their forehead. Kelly relaxed and nodded to the firefighter.

"Sorry."

"I'm just glad to get you to safety. I'll be with you the whole way. Close your eyes if you want."

"I'm fine now."

Their stretcher started up the slope.

"Let the people on top know they don't like to be touched."

"They?"

"It's complicated and not my story to tell. Just tell them to take it slow and gentle." Blue crawled over to the other stretcher. They strapped him in and then it was his turn to make the trip up the hill.

***

"There's no reason to keep you here." The doctor smiled at him but lines of exhaustion stretched her face.

"Thank you, Dr. Li." Blue stood. His muscles were stiff but he'd felt worse. Molly had ranted at him until his phone battery died. Tom had dropped by to say he'd take care of Kelly. Blue packed away the night before as something to deal with later and took a taxi up to the motel.

"You look like shit," Sasha waved a beer at him as Blue stumbled from the taxi to his room.

"Home!" Blue forced himself to take a long shower then flopped on the bed. There was a knock at the door getting him up a few minutes later.

"Harley wanted to make sure you were okay." Rod looked over his shoulder into the room while Blue greeted the dog.

"Thanks, Rod. I'm going to sleep. It's been a rough couple days." Blue closed the door and fell back on the bed.

Knocking woke him again and Blue staggered to the door. Kelly waited outside.

"Come on in." Blue stepped back. Kelly sat in a chair by the tiny table as Blue closed the door.

"I need to talk to you." They stared at the table and rubbed a crack with their thumb. "I know it's not the best time, but if I don't do it now, I'll never have the courage."

Blue sat across from Kelly who didn't look up.

"I'm here when you're ready."

"I know." Kelly rubbed their eyes, "I didn't put any makeup on; I knew I'd end up crying."

"Crying's not a weakness." Blue rolled his shoulders, "I've done my fair share."

"Okay." Kelly took a deep breath, then didn't say anything while Blue felt his heart beat. They lifted their head, "I think I'm in love with you and I have no idea what to do with that."

Blue tried to find something to say which wouldn't sound flippant or off-putting.

"I don't think I can afford this," Kelly's voice caught. "My job is everything to me and yet..." they jumped forward to kiss Blue.

When they stopped to pull back, Blue put a hand on Kelly's cheek. "I'll be here when you're ready." He planted a kiss their forehead.

Kelly gazed at Blue for a long breath, "I know, that's part of what scares me." They bolted out the door.

Blue touched his lips and his fingers came away tinted red. He guessed lipstick was waterproof. After washing his face Blue fell back on the bed.

"Well Blue, what are you going to do now?" He stared at the ceiling without the slightest hint of an answer.

Since sex education classes in school, Blue had known he wasn't 'right'. The stuff the other boys giggled over left him cold. One brought a Playboy stolen from his father. As the others snickered at the pictures, Blue tried to see what they did but all he saw were not-that-impressive pictures of women.

Since then, Blue had stood on the sidelines of the world of sex. He had friends he'd say he loved but felt no reaction from his body...nothing. So he'd lived with his mother, become a cop, then an alcoholic and then...

Blue sighed. Like Kelly he had no idea what to do with his feelings. His body was dead as ever, but his arms missed Kelly's weight and warmth. His heart wished they'd stayed but he had no idea of what would come next.

While he was awake, he called Molly.

"What does it feel like to be in love?" he asked and her mouth dropped open and her eyes looked ready to fall out.

"What? What?" Molly shook her head. "Where did that come from? Did you hit your head harder than they thought?"

Blue laughed, "It's complicated. I'll explain when you get here tomorrow — eleven, right?"

"You'd better be there."

"I will be."

Molly blew him a kiss and signed off.

"What is going on?" he laughed as he pictured Molly's face. She always teased him about 'getting out'. That discussion wasn't one he knew how to start but Molly wouldn't let him out of it. Blue smiled. Molly proved he could love — it wasn't his heart that didn't work.

After plugging in his cell and setting the alarm, he crawled back into bed

***

The stab of something in his arm woke him up. His eyes opened but wouldn't focus. Four shapes had invaded his room. Blue fought for consciousness but his eyes wouldn't cooperate. Glass broke and heat stretched the skin on his face.

They dragged him out and tossed him in the back of a van.

Molly! Kelly!

Chapter 13

Monday, June 14

Molly walked through the sun to the terminal. As much as she loved her grandmother, Kamloops was home in a way Calgary would never be. Her nosed turned up at the reek smoke in the air.

She scanned the crowd for Blue but didn't see him. The flight was a bit early. He'd be there by the time she collected her luggage.

When she was the last from her flight still waiting, Molly swore and went to find a taxi.

He'd promised. *He's been in a car crash! ...but he promised. What the hell was that talk about love? If he was with some...* Molly couldn't imagine it. He was the most loving person she'd ever met, but from the beginning he'd seen her, not her body. Acid burned a hole in her stomach as she vacillated between anger and fear.

When the driver pulled up at the motel, the yellow caution tape screamed at her. Fire had blackened a section of the motel.

Firefighters rolled a covered body from a room
Blue
The strength left her and she slumped to the asphalt, howling in wordless grief.

"You must be Molly." Someone stood beside her. "Tom, give me a hand, we can't leave her here."

Two people walked her to a room with a couch for her to fall on.

"Listen Molly, Blue isn't in there — just booze bottles, a burned-up computer and a cellphone."

"He's alive?" Molly lifted her head and her heart started beating again.

"He's not in the room. If whoever did this wanted him dead, he'd be there."

"Blue saved my life," Molly rasped. "Again and again. I'm going to find him, and anyone who gets in my way better run."

"I'm impressed!" Someone sat beside her and put an arm tentatively around her shoulders. "Anything I can do to help — you've got it."

Molly lifted her head to look at the person beside her. Her brain refused to put a gender on the person. *"To hell with it."* "I'm Molly, Blue's daughter."

"Kelly. I'm Blue's — friend."

"You're the one he was talking about last night."

"Talking about?" Kelly blushed and slid farther away.

"He asked me what it felt like to be in love. As if I'd know!" Molly laughed as tears ran down her cheeks. "I've been waiting for months to hug him."

Kelly hesitantly moved to put their arms around Molly. Molly clutched at Kelly and gave up trying to hold back the sobs.

After what felt like an eternity, Molly sat up and took a shaky breath.

"You give amazing hugs, like Blue."

To Molly's shock, Kelly burst into tears. Molly

Alex McGilvery

wrapped them in a hug until they shuddered and laughed.

"You too."

"We're going to find him," Molly said.

"Damn right!"

"Sorry — I'm the motel manager, Mr. Basu. Mr. Blue would never cause such a fire. Always polite and friendly."

"That's my dad!" Molly grinned at him and scrubbed at her face.

Mr. Basu handed her a tissue, "You need water?"

"If you don't mind," Molly nodded. *Never hurts to let someone help you,* — one of Blue's sayings.

"I brought your luggage in, Miss." A man in jeans and a t-shirt smiled at her.

"Thank you." Molly tried not to giggle at being called 'Miss.'

"That's Tom, my associate," Kelly said.

For some reason, Tom blushed deep red.

"How about if we go have lunch and do some plotting?" Kelly lifted an eyebrow.

"Sounds like a plan." Molly stood and took one suitcase while Tom pulled the other one.

"Thank you, Mr. Basu." She turned and smiled at him, "You've been very kind."

***

"I was so angry at Blue that I didn't see much more than fire and body." Molly sipped at her Coke. "I'm glad to meet you both."

"Blue was very helpful, it is the least we can do."

"Molly," Kelly blushed and peered into her drink, "Blue's the first person to hold me since…well, in far too long. He's changed my life and I barely know him. I'm not going to let him go easily."

"So what's the plan, boss?" Tom leaned back, a bemused look on his face. Kelly blushed and took a long drink, "You may have promoted me but you're still the boss."

"Right then, check with the Fire Commissioner's investigator. See if you can walk through with her if she's looking at the scene soon. Pick her brain, that woman knows fire in a way I've never imagined."

"Got it! I'll take a taxi down and rent another car."

"Put it on my account," Kelly said. "Thanks, Tom."

He nodded and left.

"It's like I've woken up in a different world," Kelly said. "He was my 'assistant' and put up with me keeping him at a distance and treating him like crap. Now I look at him and see a friend."

"Blue will do that to you." Molly pulled up her sleeve to show Kelly the scars from her drug days. "Blue got between me and my pimp — that caused him no end of trouble. At first, I hung around only because he didn't want sex and he fed me. Then, because I felt safe with him. Then he almost died saving me, and let me be his daughter. I've been in Calgary since September, at a program for girls getting off the street. His mom runs it and she's almost as amazing as he is."

Molly put out her hand, "Any friend of Blue's is a friend of mine."

"Thanks Molly." Kelly took her hand, not to shake it, but more like squeeze. "Let's get you a place to live, then we'll take it from there."

"I don't want to stay in that motel. I couldn't stand looking at that burned out room every day but I want to be in the area so I can talk with other people who are around and maybe pick up some hints of what he's been up to."

"Good thinking." Kelly dropped two fifties on the table and led the way out of the restaurant.

They drove to a few different motels in the area, finally finding one. It looked more upscale than Blue's, but felt cold. Molly used the tail end of her bank account to rent the room for the month and Kelly covered the damage deposit with their credit card.

"I will pay you back as soon as I get a job."

"No rush." Kelly looked around the room, "Not bad, but not great."

"I've lived in worse." Molly shoved her suitcases in a corner and flopped on a bed. "Sorry... suddenly I'm exhausted."

"That's all right." I've put my card on the desk. Call me when you're ready. I'd like to check in with you tomorrow if you don't mind."

"Kelly," Molly lifted a hand "...thanks. I don't know what I would have done if you weren't here."

"You would have cried for a bit, then gone out and kicked ass." Kelly left, the door clicking shut behind her.

Molly phoned the police to report Blue missing. When she said he was missing from the motel fire, the woman officer told her to stay put and they'd send someone to talk to her.

The cop on the other side of the door when Molly opened it for him, gave her a crick in the neck from staring up at him.

"I'm Constable Post," the man said. "First tell me your name."

"I'm Molly Callister. I'm twenty-one, I think."

"You think?" the officer raised an eyebrow.

"I was abandoned. They had to guess at my age. The date on my birth certificate is September 14, 1998."

What can you tell me about this?" he looked at his notes. "Blue...what's his last name?"

"He's just Blue," Molly wiped tears from her face. "He'd never burn a room like that."

"How would you know?"

"I'm his daughter." Molly set her chin and dared the officer to say anything but he only made a note. He read her the description they had of Blue. "Anything you can add?"

"No," Molly drew a shuddering breath, "I just returned to town from school. It would have been the first time I've seen him since Christmas."

"Sorry, Miss." Constable Post put his book away. "I will add to the BOLO. If any member sees him, they will bring him in for questioning. Whether he set the fire or not, we need to ask him about it."

Chapter 14

Tuesday, June 15

Molly's sleep was disturbed by noise in the hallway, but she rolled over and ignored it.

Light came through the thin curtains and she pushed herself up.

"Damn!" Molly had a cool shower and chose her clothes for the day to make her look weak and vulnerable. Whether Blue's neighbours sympathized with her or attacked her, she'd learn something. Before she dressed Molly went through a quick warm up. The Judo training facility across the street from the 'school' had become a place to work out her frustrations. Keeping the secret from Blue had just about killed her but she wanted to surprise him.

Pushing back the tears, she set her jaw, then headed out to go over to Blue's motel. The area was still taped up but a small crowd peered over it at the burned out rooms.

"...fire in a drunken rage..." a woman's voice ground on Molly's nerves, "...probably learned that freak didn't have what he expected."

"At least this time, I got my game system out." The soft looking young man was still wearing mismatched pajamas and fuzzy slippers.

"Bully for you." the woman sneered. "If you'd been paying more attention, maybe the fire wouldn't have killed Sasha."

"Knock it off, Wanda." Another tired looking woman appeared ready to smack Wanda. "Everyone knew Sasha drank himself into a stupor at night. How's Simon supposed to break down a door and pull out a full-grown man?"

Simon didn't look too pleased to be cast as a weakling kid, but he kept his mouth shut. The speculation turned back to why Blue would burn his motel room. Not one person considered it might not have been him. The odds on favourite was being dumped, or dumping Kelly.

"I heard she was trying to get him a settlement even though he had no insurance," Wanda took up her attack again.

"Don't be stupid." A cold flat voice came from behind her and something warm and wet slurped at her hand. "Insurance companies are heartless machines. She was playing him."

Wanda stepped forward as if to intimidate the short black man. A vibration at Molly's side made her hair stand on end. Wanda paled and walked away.

"You must be Harley," Molly crouched to pet the dog.

"Don't touch my dog." The dog's owner, Rod, Blue had said, glared at her. Molly backed away as Rod and Harley stalked away.

"Who are you?" Simon peered at her suspiciously.

"I'm Molly, Blue's daughter."

"Sucks to be you!" Simon wandered away.

"Blue was the only decent one down at this end."

Molly turned to see a Filipino woman in a maid's uniform. "Did you talk to him much?"

"We aren't supposed to talk to the guests unless there's a problem but he smiled at me and thanked me after I'd made up his room."

"He's like that," Molly smiled, "...has a gift for seeing people."

The maid nodded and went back to the cart of sheets and towels.

Molly headed off to the A&W for breakfast. The place was filled with groups of older people some reading papers, others talking animatedly. Two women in the corner played cards.

Molly picked up her meal and sat in a corner to eat.

"Haven't seen you here before." A tall woman with silver hair smiled at her.

"I've been away at school for the past year. My name's Molly. Somehow, I missed connections with my father," Molly shrugged. "I'll manage until I find him."

"Oh dear me!" the woman put a hand on her chest. "You are so brave. Where are you staying?"

"I'm in a motel for the moment. It isn't home, but it's shelter."

"Where did your father live?"

"Oh, his apartment burned in a fire a few weeks back."

"I read about that in the paper. If you need someone to talk to, I have breakfast here every day." The woman nodded gracefully and walked back to a table with other women of various shapes and colours, but all old.

They leaned forward and whispered. A couple glanced over at Molly; either speculation or pity in their eyes.

When Molly'd finished her food, she left, waving at

the table of women and smiling. Who knows — they could be allies and it was weirdly comforting to know someone worried about her.

***

The building inspector had no problem putting on the tyvek suit but he'd brought his own mask.

"This is much better than the cloth ones you have," Will wore work pants and a t-shirt with a graphic so worn Tom couldn't read it.

Once they both resembled aliens, the restoration company led them to Tara's suite.

"If you need to get in other apartments, come and get me."

"Sure thing."

Will moved methodically through the apartment occasionally poking at the wall with a screwdriver.

"See here? Crack in the firewall to the next apartment. They slapped plaster over it but that wasn't enough to stop the fire." Tom closed his eyes.

"There's a bedroom on the other side; a bed pushed up against the wall — had a bedskirt." He opened his eyes, "...wouldn't take much to start on the other side."

"Let's look at the balcony." Will pushed the door aside, "Must have been open." He put an arm out to stop Tom. "Concrete could be weak from the fire; don't take chances. With all this stuff on the balcony, the fire spread here too. Doesn't matter how good your wall is if the fire can go around it."

They checked the kitchen but the floor and ceiling were solid. "It went over the balcony; the windows are wood — wouldn't take long."

"Let's check the basement," Will stayed near the wall on the stairs and Tom copied him.

Will pushed into the boiler room and took out a flashlight. It lit the room like a floodlight. Tom followed him, withholding his questions, not that Will looked to be easily influenced.

"Shit!" Will pointed at some pipes with their covering hanging down, "Wasn't fire did that. Someone was looking for asbestos and struck gold."

He walked back up the stairs and out to the restoration company.

"You've got asbestos in the basement — looks disturbed. Change your protocol."

The woman with the clipboard dropped it and pulled out her cell phone, "We have a problem."

"Thanks, Will." Tom crumpled the paper mask and tossed it in the garbage, then followed it with the tyvek. "Send me your report and the bill."

"Got it." Will climbed into his truck and drove off.

Tom left the restoration people arguing over the phone. He sat in his car and called Kelly. "We have a shitstorm on the horizon. Asbestos in the basement — could be through the whole building. Flaws in at least one firewall." He listened to Kelly's response and nodded. "Sure thing, Boss. You'll have my report by noon. Will's coming as soon as he writes. He doesn't look to be the kind of person who wastes time."

After he hung up, Tom sat and thought for a while. The restoration people strung caution tape across the entrance and looked to be settling into guard duty.

Tom made another call.

"Security please."

"Tom Hintle with Kelly Pashe," Tom closed his eyes and sighed. Kelly would rip him a new one when they found out.

"Right...thanks. Yes, the apartment building fire in Kamloops. The situation has changed. I think we need some backup. Keep it discreet — I like my job."

He hung up and considered for a few seconds letting Kelly know but shook his head. They didn't like the security division and after recent events, Kelly might be even more volatile.

***

Kelly felt a shiver run down their spine. The advantage of working for a soulless corporation was that it did no good to try to interfere with their work. They just hoped whoever was out there knew that too.

Kelly didn't like feeling helpless, but they were more accountant than detective. For all the big words to Molly, they were out of her depth. Uncovering fraud was a far cry from rescuing someone.

They looked at their phone, then put it away. Time to start trusting Tom to do his part of the job and get on with theirs. Opening the computer, Kelly dug into the numbers. Tracking down the owner would help point them in the right direction.

How many times had she told Tom to be patient?

"Patience, Kelly, patience!"

97

Chapter 15

Molly sat with Tom and Kelly in a corner of Earls; the chatter of other conversations acting like a wall to protect them.

"The tenants all seem to hate each other," Molly drew circles on the table with a bit of water. "At least the ones near my father's apartment. They hung around the burned place like vultures."

"Trouble can do that..." Tom leaned back, "...either bring people together or tear them apart."

"They didn't come across as the kind to come together. Blue told me they were ganging up on a young woman they blamed for the fire." Molly said.

"Wonder what will happen when they learn it was arson?" Kelly tapped a finger on the table.

"Probably blame Blue. They're halfway there now. Not one considered any other possibility." Molly frowned and glanced at Kelly, "The reasons they came up with weren't pleasant."

"I can guess," Kelly put a hand on Molly's arm, "It's nothing I'm not used to."

"Blue'd say you shouldn't have to be used to it," Molly dabbed at her eyes with the napkin.

"He's right but it doesn't change anything," Kelly sighed, then flipped their hand. "Tom has found that the building was in much worse shape than the owner stated on their claim, not the kind of things you'd notice until too late. The management company is doing their job. They opened the books on the building for me. They collected rent and sent the money on, minus their fee. The owner had their own people doing the work."

"People who wouldn't see things they were told not to see," Tom nodded. "I'm doing some checking but without invoices, it is hard to track them down."

"The repairs were adequately done so the company didn't pursue the issue."

"Maybe the tenants know," Molly closed her eyes.

"How are you going to get them to talk to you?" Kelly looked worried.

"You'd be surprised what people will tell someone they despise." Molly drew in a breath, "I knew all kinds of secrets when I worked. The bosses wanted them as much as the money I brought in."

"I can't imagine what you've been through," Kelly squeezed Molly's arm.

"Trust me, you don't want to, and I had it easy compared to some."

"Feed what you find to Tom. You have his number, right?"

Molly shoved the memories aside. "I do."

"I'll keep digging. Listen for anyone who sounds like they came into money."

"I think some of the friction came from a few having insurance, most didn't."

"I can follow up on that," Kelly rubbed their eyes. "Tom will tell you I always counsel patience but there's never been someone's life on the line."

"I agree with you there," Tom drank from his water

glass, crunching the bits of ice. "I will talk more to the restoration company. If they think they're caught in something shady, they may give up some information."

"Whoever is behind this has a problem. There have been four deaths connected in some way to the fire. That may be why there isn't a body in the room. Blue needs to be out of touch for a while before they do anything." Kelly winced, "Sorry, that sounded cold."

"Blue would have said the same thing," Molly smiled crookedly. "A painful truth is better than a pleasant lie. But we can use that — keep the pot simmering enough to keep them worried."

"You can't be seen to be stirring the pot." Tom leaned forward. "These aren't nice people. If they feel threatened, they'll bite."

"I have a weak right foot because of people who were going to sell me to pimps in Vancouver. Blue is the first nice person I ever met. No risk is too great to bring him home." Molly tamped down the fire in her heart. These people were trying to help.

"Okay," Kelly sighed and patted Molly's hand. "But let's make sure there is a 'you' for Blue to come home to." She dug a phone out of her purse, "Use this phone to check in with us. It's got encryption nobody's going break this year or next."

The phone was a boring older model iPhone. Molly turned it on.

'Authorization number' counted down from thirty. Kelly tapped in a sequence of numbers.

"Encryption is no good if you leave the door open.

Think of a phrase at least twenty-one letters lon
can remember. That will be the password
encrypted side of the phone."

Molly nodded and took the phone and typed in her phrase. Repeated it when asked. The phone turned off and a few seconds later it buzzed: *Authorization*. Molly typed in her code with no mistakes.

A new screen came up: *Password*. She followed Kelly's prompts to create a password.

"Use the password to use it as normal, you can take pictures, video; whatever you need. The encrypted side runs in the background if you need to switch modes; open the app named 'Search for quality insurance'. You'll be taken to the authorization screen after you use your fingerprint"

***

Molly left the restaurant feeling bemused and a bit like she was acting in a movie. *"I'll be acting but the blood will be real."* She stopped in to leave her other phone in her room, and texted her grandmother the new number.

Back out in the smoky sunshine, Molly walked to the Panorama and the outlook Blue kept mentioning. Rod and Harley were strolling about. When they rounded a corner where they could see Molly, Harley's tail wagged. Rod snapped his fingers and Harley followed but her head turned to watch Molly as she passed.

Molly ignored them to stand looking at the view. She'd never come up here before. Crossing the bridge was forbidden when she was working. After that she didn't have the need.

The rivers gleamed like pewter, but she could barely see the outline of the mountains through the smoke. Before she'd come back, the news had been full of wild claims like *"British Columbia is burning!"* Looking at the sky, Molly could believe it. But for all the smoke, she didn't see any flames.

Chapter 16

Wednesday, June 16

Molly walked out the backdoor of the motel and paused to consider her first step.

"No smoking here." A man in blue coveralls and a broom pointed at her.

"I don't smoke."

"You all smoke," he ran his fingers through his steel coloured hair. Molly froze a second as a tattoo winked at her from his wrist. "In case you think you can complain and cause me trouble, I run this place." When he waved his hand, Molly guessed he meant more than the motel.

"I'll stay out of your way," Molly looked down as she walked away. His coveralls read 'George' but she doubted that was his name. Even if he wasn't all he claimed, he'd be dangerous.

With nothing better to do, she headed down to the motel.

"You back — again?" Wanda sneered at her.

"I can't believe my father is gone. I gotta come down to make it real every day."

"Sure. I owed your old man something. Come to my room and I'll give it to you."

Lame! How many times did she practice that in the mirror. Molly followed because she wouldn't learn anything standing in the middle of the parking lot.

Around the corner, Wanda grabbed Molly by the hair

— harder to do since she'd cut it shorter. Molly let her shoulders take the force of the wall as the other woman slammed her against it. Molly acted like she'd bounced her head hard.

Wanda punched her in the stomach and Molly obligingly leaned over, tilting her face so the knee hit her cheek and orbital bones.

Molly dropped to the ground and covered her face so Wanda wouldn't see the lack of major damage.

"You come by here again, I'll put you to work. I know a hooker when I see one."

"Takes one to know one." The words slipped past her lips and prompted a kick to the ribs.

"I got friends who could make you vanish, poof!"

Though most of the ones Molly had known were dead, she didn't doubt others had taken their place.

"Poor little girl got stupid, just like her father." Molly could hear the quotes in the air, "Disappear, or I'll help you to."

Wanda swaggered away. The woman had never planned to put Molly to work or she'd have avoided the face. Molly sat up to assess the damage; black eye, swollen cheek, but no blood. Her ribs ached but nothing cracked. She spat on the ground beside her — no blood.

Molly leaned her head against the wall. She'd taken a beating from an amateur and for what? So some wannabe could posture? If Wanda really knew people, she wouldn't be bragging about it.

A memory of George flashing his tattoo made her smile. If she got a closer look at the tat, it wouldn't be the real thing, she'd bet her bank account on it. That pair would be a great couple. Maybe Molly should arrange for them to meet.

"Holy shit! What happened to you?" Simon stared at her wide eyed.

"Ran into a post." Molly pushed herself to her feet and Simon moved to support her.

"I'll get you some ice." He looked nervously at a door at the end of the building. Harley had her nose on the railing. Simon opened the door and let Molly in.

"Sorry, I'm a slob," Simon pushed fast food bags off a chair, "I'll go get some ice."

Molly swivelled in the chair to take in the room. Both beds were a mess. A semi-circle of bare rug surrounded the game system hooked up to a big TV. Another circle of tidiness surrounded a picture on a stand. It faced the bed so Molly couldn't see it.

"Got some ice and a clean towel from one of the maids," he dumped ice into the towel and twisted it. It magically looked like the ice bags she'd seen in old movies. Simon delicately put it on Molly's cheek. She put a hand on it to hold it in place. The cool soothed the ache.

"Thanks, you're a star." Molly tried to smile but it didn't work very well with the ice bag.

"Nah — used to want to be a paramedic," Simon slumped on a bed. "Couldn't pass the physical."

"That's hard, so what's the second choice?"

"Playing video games and stuffing myself until I die."

"Wouldn't she be disappointed if you were gone?" Molly tilted her chin at the frame.

"My girlfriend — ex-girlfriend now I guess." He picked up the photo and stared at it. "She wasn't much but she was my friend. I left my game system behind to help her rescue her rabbits. Then she went back to her mom's place to live. Her mom hates me."

"Did she tell you she was leaving you?" Molly felt a strange sympathy for this overgrown child, "I wouldn't count her out until she says the words."

"Really?" Simon put the picture back on the dresser, arranging it carefully and dusting the bare wood around it. He slumped on the bed, "Nah — she hates me."

"Simon, do you give up when you die in a game?"

"No, everybody dies, it's part of the game. My life isn't a game; there's no reset button."

"Not reset, no, but it doesn't mean we're supposed to give up at the first setback. A lot of life is like grinding levels; boring as hell but it has to be done."

Simon stared at her, mouth open.

"What?" Molly glared at him.

"He said the same thing." Simon rubbed his face. "He went off to work somewhere every day like he had a purpose."

"That's my father!" Molly couldn't help the pride in her voice. "He's been through even more hell than me, but he still helps people."

"I should have listened to him." He sighed and curled into a ball on the bed. Molly had the feeling he'd never move again.

"It isn't too late to listen." Molly stood over him and squeezed ice water from the towel on him.

"What the f—!"

"Do you *want* to be a helpless slob?"

"No," He curled tighter. "But I can't change. I've tried."

She dumped the ice over him. He sat up sputtering.

"Life is hard, dipshit." Molly made her words cut into him, "I was a hooker and an addict. People were trying to kill me or sell me. If I'd moaned that I couldn't change, I'd be dead."

"Dead?" Simon sat in the ice, water streaking down his face.

"Dead in a ditch and no one to give a shit."

She took a deep breath, *"Why am I taking my shit out on this kid?"* Molly opened her mouth to apologize.

"How did you do it?" His eyes looked like they belonged to a puppy.

"How? Because it was that or die. It was the hardest thing I've ever done, but I didn't want to die. Blue helped me at the exact moment I needed a reason to live."

"Helped you?"

"He told me life was my choice, then refused to make decisions for me, but he got shot saving me." Molly brushed at the tears stinging her swollen cheek. "No one can decide for you, but make the decision and there will be people who will help."

"Would you help?"

"As much as I can. I'll be your big sister from hell. But I'm not the best person." She picked up the photo and held it out to Simon, "This girl gave you the same thing Blue gave me — the right to choose your life."

Simon snatched the photo from her.

"Fran?" He rubbed the frame with his thumb, "Is that what you meant? Where do I start?"

"Make a list of the things you know you should be doing. Then do the last thing you want. Again tomorrow, believe if you give up, you will die. Failure will happen but get up and get back to work. When you have that one nailed, pick the next last thing on that list."

Simon had a burger bag and was scribbling on it. "Shit! I'm going to need some garbage bags to clean this mess. Will I see you again?" The puppy eyes returned.

"Friday, at the A&W, at eight in the morning. I'll be eating breakfast there." Molly stood and started to pick her way to the door.

"Molly." Simon jumped up. "Your dad, someone took him. They had a black van. That's all I saw."

"Thank you, Simon," Molly smiled and went out the door.

"So you're giving it away for free now?" Wanda's face twisted.

"My boss is going to be curious about my face; doesn't like to lose money. You're Wanda, right? Don't want to get the name wrong." Molly stepped around the woman who had frozen like a pillar of salt.

Mr Basu came out of the office a worried look on his face.

"My dear, what happened?"

"Nothing you need to worry about, Mr. Basu. I'm fine."

Molly hoped Simon's resolve would hold but the look

of terror on Wanda's face made her feel dirty. With any luck she wouldn't run into any more trouble on the way to the shower.

She passed Rod and Harley. The dog turned her head.

"Front," Rod spoke quietly, but Harley's nose snapped to the front.

A long cold shower, then a few exercises to loosen her muscles made Molly feel better.

The bruises were showing purple and yellow. Shallow, most of the colour would be gone in a day or so. She shouldn't shock the ladies at A&W too badly.

Molly sat at the desk and made a list of what she knew. It was depressing. Someone with a black van took Blue. They were assuming it was connected to the fire, but Blue had his enemies too. Kelly could look into Wanda and George, but they were almost certainly wannabes.

She lay on the bed and closed her eyes, wishing Blue was there to dump a bucket of ice on her.

***

Kelly sat at the computer and swore at it. The labyrinth, hiding where the money went, looked to be unbreakable. If they had unlimited access and time, maybe. The payout would be to the management company; they'd keep their fee and the rest would vanish. Kelly didn't like the idea of some anonymous person getting her company's money, especially if it might be fraud.

The officer's report from the Fire Commissioner's office said grease fire, but didn't quite suggest arson. They couldn't think of a mechanism. Right now, that was the important angle to attack. A hint of evidence of arson and the head office would slam the door.

They opened a new tab and typed in *"grease fires"*. Time to see what craziness the Internet was up to.

***

Tom sat back and hit enter. This was a total fishing trip and might even cost the company money but if it worked it would be worth it. He'd heard of the police pulling similar scams. Looking at the jobs available became a temptation too powerful to resist. It happened every time he stepped a bit too far.

The first time it had been literal; it was his first job with Kelly. They had a reputation in the office. Cold, strict, terrifying. He had to agree with the rumours. Kelly asked, he jumped. This was a big step up for him and he wasn't going to blow it.

While Kelly had coffee with the owners of a new building that had collapsed under the weight of snow, Tom was told to find the roof trusses in question and get as many photos as he could.

A cranky woman in well-worn work pants and a white hard hat walked him up through areas blocked off with caution tape. He had steel toes on and a hard hat that didn't want to fit.

"That's the last of 'em. The rest are trashed."

"Is there a way I can get a closer look?"

"Suppose you put a harness on and walk out there."

"Well, let's get the stuff and do this."

The woman looked at him in shock but whistled and a crew of men appeared as if by magic.

They fitted him what they called a fall harness.

Columbia Smoke

"It'll save your life but won't keep your shorts clean."

Tom wrapped the strap of the camera around his wrist and had a worker zip tie it. He wasn't going to do something this crazy and not have pictures to show for it.

Walking out on the truss was the easy part. It was wider than the curbs he walked as a kid, no busses roaring past to startle him.

The hard part was stopping, crouching, taking pictures, then standing up to go farther out.

He'd reached the end of the pulley track for his harness and heard a distinct creak from under him. Tom sat on the beam with a leg on each side. He leaned forward to hold the camera beneath the truss, but couldn't reach. He took a deep breath then tilted to the side. The transition to hanging upside down, held only by his not-very-muscular legs, came far too quickly. But as his hard hat rattled in the wreckage below, Tom zoomed in and took pictures of the flaw in the beam. He waved when he'd finished, and they hoisted him upright on the beam. The walk back was easy.

Back on the ground, Kelly and the exec's met him.

"What were you doing?" they asked.

"I was told that was the last one in place."

"Did you get the pictures?

Tom handed them the camera after his guide cut the zip-tie.

While Kelly had dinner with the execs, the construction crew took him to a bar and did their best to get him drunk.

A month after that, as he wrote endless reports trying

not to make himself look like the reckless idiot he was, Kelly stopped at his desk.

"Here," they dropped a paper on his desk, "We have an assessment next week. Monday, 6 a.m., a car will pick you up." They left, and Tom looked at the paper. It was an industrial safety course which would qualify him in using fall protection, basic enclosed space work, and a few others he wasn't sure about.

They'd worked as a team in the five years since then.

***

Blue coughed on the smoke but someone put a can in his hand so he drank it down. Tasted like crap, but beer was beer. He got tired so he put the can down and went to sleep on the floor.

"There's something I should remember…"

Chapter 17

Thursday, June 17

Once again people ran up and down the hall late into the night. They might have been throwing a party in several rooms. Someone tried her door, and Molly sat up and called the front desk.

"There are people making a huge racket. I'm in room 320 — yes — please send someone up to ask them to be quiet."

Banging woke her. There was yelling for 'quiet'. *Finally.*

She left early to avoid George and didn't truly relax until she was out of shouting distance of the motel. Coffee at Starbucks had become an expensive habit. Maybe it was time to get a job to pay for these luxuries but not until she had Blue back.

Molly wiped her eyes annoyed with herself for letting the tears out again. She could take a beating and not bat an eye, but think about Blue and she became a fountain.

The world wasn't as safe a place without him. She drew a shuddering breath and reached for her coffee. This is what she got for thinking in the morning. Her hand bumped into a tin like they used for gift cards. Inside was a hastily scribbled note.

It read, "If you need help, come order another coffee and we'll get you to a shelter."

There were good people in the world. They may not

have gone through what she had but they had their own stories. She wouldn't die if Blue didn't make it back, though she'd probably wish she could. Her life goal was to be one of the good ones. Molly slipped the tin and the note into her pocket and looked up at the man at the till.

"Thank you," she mouthed, then concentrated on her coffee. Kelly pulled into the parking lot and the lineup at the till was too long to chat with the server. Another time. Molly waved and smiled as she left.

"Good God, girl! What were you doing?" Tom twisted to stare at her as Molly climbed into the back seat.

"Getting information." Molly grinned and her cheek ached.

"I'm surprised people weren't phoning the police," Kelly frowned at her.

"They did better than that. I'll tell you about it."

Kelly drove them to the Denny's on the north shore.

"Order whatever you want."

"At least the baseball didn't hit my teeth," Molly laughed, "so I can chew the steak." She caught the relief on the server's face.

Their breakfasts arrived and Molly tucked in to her steak and eggs. She'd never eaten this much in the morning.

"Smart thinking," Kelly smiled. "Don't want the staff getting worried about you."

"Now what were you really doing?" Tom leaned forward.

Molly filled them in on her information.

"Can we trust what this Simon said? He may have been trying to impress you." Tom frowned.

"I don't think so," Molly cut another piece of steak. "He's fixated on his girl. I'm a scary woman he'll probably be glad to never see again."

"What made you decide to go full intervention on him?" Kelly asked and ran a piece of pancake through the syrup on their plate.

"He risked a lot to help me. Or he believed he did, which amounts to the same thing. And Blue wanted to help him."

"Fair enough but a black van isn't much to go on." Tom finished his fruit and yoghurt and pushed the bowl away.

"I get it, just a tiny piece of the puzzle. We push it aside until it is important. The big thing is that two people have said that Blue was taken."

"Two people?" Tom screwed up his face.

"Wanda. When she was sneering at Molly," Kelly speared another bit of pancake.

"Right," Tom took a long drink of coffee.

"One other thing," Molly pushed the remnants of her meal away, "Wanda was terrified that I might know a 'boss'. Interfering in a gang's cashflow is a sure way to get their attention. Stay away from drugs and girls and they won't care."

"So if someone got into shady real estate, the gang wouldn't do anything?"

"Why bother? It would be risk for no return. The most they might do is try to launder money through it."

"Doesn't have the feel of laundering; the tenants and the money are real. Where's the extra cash?"

"What if we're dealing with wannabe's?" Molly leaned forward, then changed her mind. Another meal like that and her jeans wouldn't fit.

"Wannabes?"

"People who want to be tough but take the easy way."

"Like someone who buys a Harley and leather and only rides it around the neighbourhood." Kelly elbowed Tom.

"Coleen just wanted a bike. She rides it to work every day — says it keeps the staff in line." Tom frowned.

"Coleen runs a daycare," Kelly whispered to Molly behind her hand.

"So anyway, where do we go from here?" Tom's face was red.

"We follow through on your sting. The VP even said we could pay out a little if we don't go overboard. This claim could run into millions and if we have any other properties insured by the same client…" Kelly shook their head.

"Do you have any other buildings with this client?" Molly's stomach was settling down. Years of abusing it on the street had made it tough.

"Unless there is a series of claims, we don't usually investigate other properties. There are privacy issues, and we don't have the time."

"Makes sense," Molly nodded.

"I'll check with the VP anyway." Kelly tapped on her phone, then replaced it face down on the table.

"I can't remember the last investigation that went on this long." Tom looked to have recovered his aplomb.

"There was that flood one a few years back but that was more sheer volume, not our normal job." Kelly rolled her eyes, "Normally, we get the ones that might be a high settlement but also involve a client we don't want to insult."

"Kelly crawls through the financials and I crawl through everything else," he laughed. "I remember our first investigation. I had to get photos of the one beam that hadn't collapsed."

"So, he harnessed up and walked on the thing to get the pictures. I'm on my way out and see a hard hat falling. There's Tom hanging upside down from the beams taking photos. Then he's up, and walks cool as a cucumber back to safety," Kelly chuckled. "I decided then I wanted him as a partner."

"Because I was crazy?" Tom's eyebrows rose.

"Not at all. You made sure you were safe. You got the job done and didn't make a fuss about it. Coleen's the one who likes crazy. I wanted someone I could trust at my back."

"I...you never told me that before."

"I never thought to." Kelly looked down, "I thought my thinking was obvious. Tom has certification to go up, over, under, through just about anything you can imagine."

"Helps to have a wife who's a construction lead hand."

"Remember when you wanted to check that manure tank? They were all about safety this and that. So Tom pulls out his wallet, thumbs through a stack of cards and comes up with an enclosed space certification."

"All I found was that they'd been doing all the maintenance required which matched their records. They really were just worrying about me."

"Yup. We got a nice bonus for that one. It was a fair payout and the client brought all their insurance over to us."

"Sounds interesting, maybe if social work doesn't work out, I can get a job with you."

"You have the right mind set: detail oriented; don't jump to conclusions."

"And you're patient." Tom interjected, and he and Kelly laughed.

"But no more getting beat up for information," Kelly waggled a finger.

"What about dumping ice on a client?" Molly grinned at her.

"Depends on whether the client needed an ice bath," Kelly grinned back.

"Look, while we're here, do you mind if I check out a couple thrift stores? Penny Pinchers is just on the corner."

"No problem. Text me when you're done."

***

When the door closed behind Molly, Tom leaned forward.

"Are you okay?" His gut told him to shut up, but he ignored it, "As pleasant as it is to travel down memory lane, you've never been like this before."

Kelly stared into their coffee until Tom's heart threatened to quit.

"I've always been different. My parents thought I was cursed and my classmates teased me, so I thought the only way to live was by being detached. If I didn't care, then it didn't matter." Kelly reached out a hand to Tom, then withdrew it. "You were the first person to ever simply accept me. Even talking to others, you didn't call me names. You and Coleen had me at your wedding. I thought you were the only one."

They dabbed at their eyes. Tom put his hand on theirs.

"I was terrified of you, then I worshipped you. Now, you are my friend and I feel privileged to say that."

"Thank you. I, too, am privileged," Kelly tried to smile and failed. "After I crashed the car, I had a freak out — full blown, all out, losing my shit. Blue came to help me and I backhanded him. You know what he said? 'A slap is a small price to pay to have you calm again.'" Kelly looked at Tom with wet eyes, "He saved me and kept me warm right through until we were rescued. Never once did he blame me. I might have killed both of us."

"I've known for a long time that you built a wall to keep people at a safe distance. I didn't know what I'd do if it ever cracked but Coleen told me I'd better be there for you."

"What do I do now?" Kelly rubbed their eyes and snorted. "If I'm going to cry this much, I'll have to get better mascara."

"They do sell waterproof," Tom said and Kelly laughed.

"I'll be back in a moment." And they headed for the washroom.

"Is your…" the server trailed off.

"My friend is fine. It's been a rough few days." Tom smiled at him.

Kelly returned looking as cool as ever.

"While we are talking," Tom swallowed, "I have a confession to make."

"You called security," Kelly slid into her seat. "Why do you think I gave her a company phone? One thing I've learned is to trust you. That other time was my pride speaking. I would have apologized but I didn't know how."

"You just did, very nicely too," Tom laughed. "They weren't sure what to do with Molly. Ban's comment was that she knew how to take a beating. I think it was a compliment."

"I'll let you explain it to her."

"Thanks." Tom stood, "I'm guessing that buzz is Molly. Head office has never been that quick."

"You're right, she wants to know what size shirt you wear."

"Medium," Tom replied.

"I thought you'd gone down a size. Coleen is good for you," Kelly tapped the phone and then put it away. "Can you believe I've never been in a thrift store? Maybe we should remedy that."

"The one on the corner is probably where Molly is heading."

They drove the few hundred yards and parked. Kelly led the way in with an odd eagerness. Tom smiled — they were back to the cool, observant Kelly he'd worked with for years. No, they were more relaxed.

***

Molly waved as Kelly and Tom came in. She was almost done anyway. But Kelly wanted to see the whole place. Tom followed behind with a slight smile. Kelly bought themself a purple fedora. Tom was speechless at the coverall with *'Tom'* embroidered on the pocket.

"I couldn't resist," Molly grinned, "but this is the real find." She held up the wallet and let it fall open. A long accordion of cards fell out, "For your certification cards."

Tom caressed it, "I didn't think they actually made these. I've seen it in the movies. It's fantastic."

"I'd better get to work. Head office may have that information soon, and Tom, you have that sting to set up."

"The management company doesn't have space at their office but suggested I talk to the Sandman, so we have a swanky room with tea and coffee for a very reasonable price. All that's left is for me to put together paperwork for the legal eagles. They want to check that I don't sign away the company by mistake."

"I'm going to go talk to a few of Blue's friends," Molly said. "I'll catch the bus back up to the motel."

"Be careful," Kelly put their hand on Molly's shoulder.

"I will," Molly said with a twinge. "Blue told me that being careful wasn't a weakness."

"Smart man," Kelly gave her a squeeze. "We meet tomorrow for breakfast?"

"Only if it's at A&W on Columbia."

"Do you really think he'll show?" Tom looked worried.

"It doesn't matter if he doesn't show," Molly sorted through her feelings, "but I have to."

"Blue would be proud of you," Tom said. "I have the feeling he was a man to keep his word."

***

Molly pushed open the door to the LOOP and walked in. A woman waved from the kitchen and a man came over to ask Molly what she wanted to eat.

"I've already eaten enough for a week, but I wouldn't mind a coffee."

The man brought her a cup, then sat across from her. "What brings you in?"

"I wanted to talk to someone who knows Blue." She explained that he'd disappeared. Travis told her about the day he fell apart.

"He's been seeing a counsellor." Travis shrugged, "Wish I could tell you more. We'll put the word out. If anyone has seen him or heard a whisper, we'll let you know."

The people at the LOOP convinced her to join them at the Kamloops Food Council potluck. Someone told a Blue story and suddenly it felt like a wake. Molly wanted to scream at them, but she bit her cheek.

"You taking the bus? Erica asked. "I'll wait with you at the bus stop."

They walked slowly to keep from straining Erica's knees.

"It isn't that they have given up on him," Erica said after she'd lowered herself to the bench. "But folks come and go so fast on the street that it's less painful to let go than hang on."

"I guess I get that but I'm going to hang on anyway."

The bus rumbled up to the stop. "Are you going to be okay getting home?" Molly asked.

"Live in Spero House. Get on now before he drives

off."

Molly clambered on and counted change into the fare box as the driver waiting patiently.

"Thanks," Molly dropped into a seat.

"Some are all about the schedule but what's the good of being on time if you leave people standing?" The driver smiled, then drove on.

After changing busses at Landsdowne, Molly rode up Columbia. Blue had done this trip every day he'd worked. She looked out the window to see the same things he'd seen.

***

Blue put the rye bottle down. The more he drank the worse he felt. Switching to the rye hadn't helped. He explored the room. The walls were rough wood with no give in them. The one window had a steel lattice over it and was so dirty he couldn't see outside. The door was more heavy wood. If there was a way out, Blue couldn't find it.

Of course, you can't — you're drunk!

The voice in his mind stung with contempt.

"I don't remember anything."

Not until you're sober.

Blue recalled saying to someone that he and alcohol had a messy divorce — but who? It felt important but his brain wouldn't focus.

Sleep — no more drinking.

Blue curled up in the corner and closed his eyes. The bang of the door opening woke him. Two men grabbed him, twisting his arms behind him, and a third forced his head back and a bottle was shoved in his mouth.

"Drink you piece of shit. Drink or die."

Blue wanted to die rather than drink, but the inside voice told him to swallow. *"Now that you're awake, you need to live."*

Chapter 18

Molly dragged herself into the motel and stopped in shock. Her suitcases were sitting in the lobby.

The woman at the counter looked at Molly like she'd tracked dog shit into the room. "There have been too many complaints about you being noisy. Someone called a complaint last night about 320."

"That was me! I called from my room because the noise was keeping *me* awake."

"So you say." The woman only scowled more, "I don't know why they let someone like you in here in the first place but we checked out your room and found enough to evict you."

"Fine then! Give me the balance of the rent and I'm out of here."

"You get evicted; you forfeit the rent. It's in the contract."

Molly stomach reacted like she'd taken a physical blow, "I didn't sign a contract. The man didn't offer one."

"Why should I believe you? Get your crap and get out of here or I'll have the police come and clear you out."

Molly briefly considered calling the woman's bluff but with her brown face, bruises and tracks, even if they were old, a night in a cell might be the best outcome.

Burning with shame, and anger, Molly took the suitcases and walked out.

Now what? A simple phone call to Kelly felt impossible.

Would Kelly even believe her?

Molly dragged her bags to the tiny outlook and looked for a place she could crash. The lights of Kamloops any other time would have entranced her.

She'd never slept cold without Blue. Her knees lost all strength and she collapsed weeping.

"Miss." the voice persisted until Molly looked up, still gasping for breath. "It isn't safe here. Bad people come at night. Come into the office." The woman put out a hand, "It will be safer to talk inside."

Molly took the hand, and they dragged her bags into the office of the nearby motel.

The woman took a bottle of water from the fridge and opened it for Molly. "I am Ruchi, the manager's niece. He would fire me if I left you out there."

"I don't have any money. They wouldn't give it back. It was all I had," Molly sobbed again. Ruchi sat beside her and rubbed her back. "Come into the back room where you can be private. I must call my uncle."

Molly flaked out on the small couch and tried to think of what to do next.

"Uncle says to keep you here. We have no rooms open but this is better than the park. You get hungry, I'll share my lunch."

"Thank you," Molly sat up and wiped at her face. Ruchi handed her a white towel, "You don't even know me — why are you doing this?"

"Kindness is only in the world if we put it there."

Molly slept fitfully. People entered the outside office once or twice but only a murmur of voices made it back to her.

She woke up to see sunlight streaming into the office.

"What time is it?" Molly scrambled for her phone. "Oh God, I'm going to be late."

"It is ten to eight," Ruchi said from the front. My shift is just ending. Can I drive you somewhere?"

"I have an appointment at A&W."

"I hear it's a good place to work."

"Can I leave my bags here?" Flame travelled up Molly's face, "I have nowhere else."

"Of course. We'll keep them safe for you."

Ruchi dropped Molly at the front door of the restaurant and she ran in and stopped to scan the room but no Simon. Her shoulders slumped and tears welled up.

"Molly, my dear." The stately woman guided her to the table with the other women, "What happened?" She pulled a lacy handkerchief from her sleeve and dabbed at Molly's face.

"Never mind that," another woman handed Molly a wet wipe from her purse, "I'm Gertie."

"How rude of me!" The stately, silver haired woman introduced herself. "I am Roberta, but you can call me Bobbie."

"I swear, Bobbie, you do that just to see the looks on their faces." A different woman laughed.

"It is my name, Viv," Bobbie smiled as she sat. "The quiet ones are Katerine and Dusi."

"May I take your order?" someone stood beside Molly. She gave her face a final wipe and looked up. "I didn't think you took..." her jaw dropped and she jumped to hug

Simon tightly.

"I sold my game system and all my games," Simon awkwardly wrapped his arms around her. "I told myself I won't play again until I save enough for a new one. I called Fran to tell her."

"I only have a bit of change for coffee."

"Don't worry about it, this is on me." Simon gave her a lopsided smile. "If it wasn't for you, I wouldn't have applied for this job."

"Bring me something breakfast-shaped." Molly's brain tried to catch up with the change. He'd shaved and had his hair cut. Standing in his brown and orange uniform he didn't look so soft.

Simon returned to the back.

"Such a nice boy. Is he your boyfriend?" Viv asked, her sparkling blue eyes matched the dye in her hair.

"No, I'm his evil older sister," Molly grinned, "He has a girlfriend."

"You don't look evil," Gertie said, "but it does look like you've had a hard time."

Molly let the whole story pour out. The women didn't interrupt. At some point, Simon put her breakfast in front of her. She finally ran out of words and looked up at the women. She'd expected pity or sympathy but what she saw was anger.

"How dare they!" Dusi said. "That is absolutely wrong. They have to give you warnings and there is a process to follow. And for them to go into your room…"

"Dusi was a lawyer in Nigeria. She came over with her grandson to keep him out of trouble," Viv said.

"But he didn't get into trouble, so I got bored and studied law here. I don't intend to write the bar, though. I'm a grandmother and don't want to work that hard."

The women laughed and Molly's chest eased. These were good people.

"We get together for breakfast every day," Bobbie sipped at her orange juice, "and every once in a while we put on our pointy witch shoes and go kick ass."

"We'll have your money back before lunchtime."

"They'll do the same thing to someone else." Molly hardened her eyes, "I don't want anyone to go through what I did."

"Welcome to the Pointy Shoes Club," Bobbie smiled broadly at her. The women leaned in and started making plans.

"What have I done?" They tried out ideas from picketing the motel to buying it and firing all the staff. Molly lost track of the conversation. *"I can't let myself be distracted — Blue is out there."*

"They'll be at that all day," Katerine whispered to Molly. "Let's go get you somewhere to live where you'll be safe." She dragged Molly out of the restaurant to a car that should have been in a museum, "We're going to see a friend of mine." Katerine drove the car sedately. "Martha is a member of the Pointy Shoes but the poor dear can't get out anymore. Her family wants to move her in with one of them, but they made a deal: if she gets someone to live with her, they will let her alone."

"I don't know anything about taking care of people."

"Martha doesn't need much taking care of. You'll see

when we get there."

They collected Molly's luggage before driving the hill to pull up in front of a house that looked more like a castle than a house.

"She lives here by herself?" Molly stared at the place.

"Her husband built this house for her. He was an architect." Katerine led her up the walk, opened the front door and walked in.

"Martha, you have a visitor. Her name is Molly."

"Katerine, what a pleasant surprise!" Martha came into the room. She carried a white cane and wore elegant glasses with black lenses. "Come into the kitchen and I'll put on water for tea."

Katerine followed with a smile so Molly put aside her doubts and trailed behind them into the kitchen.

"Take one of the red chairs," Martha bustled about filling a kettle with water and plugging it in. While it heated, she pulled a plate from the fridge, "We'll have some sweets to go with the tea. I baked them yesterday."

"That sounds amazing!" Molly wanted to pull the wrap off the plate and see what kind of baking this blind lady did. She restrained herself as Martha fetched teacups and saucers to put on the table.

"I do like to use teacups but I have a hard time matching them so please excuse me if they aren't right."

"I don't think I've ever drunk tea from a teacup," Molly ran her finger around the rim. The cup looked like it would fall to pieces with a touch.

"The tea is the same," Martha said. "I use mugs when I'm on my own because it isn't such a loss if one breaks but the cups remind me of my mother."

"They are beautiful — much nicer than anything I've seen in the thrift stores."

"When my husband and I first arrived in Canada, all our furniture was bought in a second hand shop. I do hate to see waste and it was such fun imagining the stories the things could tell."

"I do that with clothes sometimes," Molly ran a finger down her sleeve. "I think I'm more comfortable in clothing with history."

"Exactly!" Martha beamed a smile at Molly and she had to remind herself the elderly woman was blind.

The teapot looked as elegant as the cups. Martha put it on the table and covered it with a tea cozy that looked like a chicken.

"Dear, do you mind if I touch your face before I sit down?"

"Not at all."

Martha put out a hand, "Take my hand and I'll follow your arm up."

Martha's touch might have been what butterflies felt like fluttering against her.

"My, what beautiful bones!" Martha froze as her fingers encountered the bruise, "Someone has been hitting you."

"Can I wait until after tea to tell you about it?"

"Of course, dear," Martha sat in her yellow chair, "how civilized of you!" She removed the chicken and gently swirled the pot. Briefly testing the position of the cups with her hand, Martha poured tea into the cups stopping comfortably short of the rim.

"After decades of pouring tea, I could pour with my eyes closed," Martha chuckled and slid the full cups and saucers toward Molly and Katerine. "Oh dear! I forgot the cream and sugar."

"It's okay. We were never allowed cream and sugar when I grew up."

"I see," Martha looked down for a moment.

"I know where everything is. You talk to Molly."

"Of course, Katerine." Martha turned to Molly, "Where did you grow up?"

"I grew up in the foster care system." Molly talked about being abandoned, the foster parents, their cruelty, and her rebellion, "I know now I was a difficult child to raise."

"You were a child — you were supposed to be difficult. Parents can't discipline a child unless they are themselves disciplined. It almost took me too long to realize that."

"I'm sorry, but I have to leave now." Katerine stood up and brushed hand across Molly's shoulder"

"Thanks for your help." Molly smiled at Katerine, then looked back at Martha. "How many children do you have?"

"I have three sons and a daughter." Martha stood, "I will go get their pictures. She walked confidently down the hall and returned with a picture frame in her hand, "This is the last picture we took as a family before I lost my sight. This is my eldest son…"

As Martha talked about her family, Molly tried to ignore a void in her chest. She had no pictures of growing up, no family portraits. Her breathe caught. Martha instantly stopped her description.

"Molly, my dear, I'm sorry. I should have thought..."

"No!" It came out stronger than Molly intended, "My life shouldn't take away the sense of family from others." Tears rolled down her cheeks, but she tried to keep her breathing even.

"You are such a kind, brave young woman." Martha slid her hand across the table until she found Molly's, then squeezed it, "I am privileged to meet you."

"You don't know my history..." Molly tried to imagine talking about her sordid past on the street in this elegant house with these women drinking from art as if it was the most normal of things.

"After the war, the people in my village were hungry. Our fields were burnt or filled with unexploded bombs. My family was hungry. There was only one person with food. I went to trade with him for food but there was only one thing he wanted, and I gave it to him, knowing I was shaming my family. When my belly swelled, the villagers were set to shear my head and turn me out. A rough farmer who rarely came to the village claimed the child was his, so we were married. He brought me here and studied to be an architect. Over sixty years we were together, and he never once treated my eldest differently from the children of his blood."

Molly looked at this aristocratic woman with her perfect hair and fine china. She understood Molly on a deeper level than almost anyone else in her life.

Katerine told me you needed someone to live with you. Please let me stay. I have so much I want to learn from you."

Chapter 19

Her room in the apartment had been bare white, with a bed and desk. At the school, it hadn't been much different. When she'd visited Grandmother, she had to move boxes around to get to the bed.

Molly stood with her jaw open in the doorway.

"Is everything okay, Molly?" Martha waited patiently behind her.

"This — I've never seen a room like this. Is the floor real wood?" She blushed at asking such a stupid question.

"You have a good eye, dear. My husband insisted on hardwood floors throughout. He had every board custom cut for the house; the same with the trim. I was happy with the tiny place we started in but he had a dream and now living in the house is like he's still here. I hope the colour is fine with you. I think it's a soft yellow but I haven't been in the other rooms for so long."

"It is yellow, it's like living inside a flower."

Martha laughed and it sounded like music.

"You'll need to take the dust sheets off and do a bit of cleaning."

"I don't mind cleaning, just show me where everything is."

"This way," Martha walked unerringly to a closet. "This is the cleaning cupboard. It is very important to put everything exactly where you got it. See the labels? Those are braille and there are print labels too."

"I get it, that's how you move around so easily. You

know where everything is and if it is moved, you'll get lost." Molly ran her fingers over the braille, "What's it like to be blind?" She put her hand over her mouth.

"Lonely," Martha said. "I would love to see the faces of my grandchildren and great grandchildren. But I am blind and complaining won't change it. I hope you don't mind chatting over tea once in a while."

"I would be delighted, but I'll be out a lot too. There are some things I need to do, and I want to get a job before starting university."

"What are you planning to take?"

"I've been accepted for social work."

"How delightful, my son teaches the statistics class for the social work course."

"I will look forward to meeting him."

Molly got to work on the room. It didn't need much more than a good polish. The dust cloths revealed plain wood furniture but somehow it looked better without decoration, as the wood grain drew pictures across every surface.

Her clothes only took three of the drawers in the six-drawer dresser and the closet was almost as big as her side of the room at the school. It looked crazy with only a few blouses hanging on the bar. Her laptop looked lonely on the large desk. Instead of the office chairs she was used to, there was a tall wingback chair. Paper, pens, and pencils filled the top drawer. An electrical plug was easily accessible if she didn't mind crawling under the desk.

Moving in with Martha had been surprisingly easy. The harder task was keeping Kelly from personally going and tearing the motel apart.

"The Pointy Shoes ladies are dealing with it," Molly put a hand on Kelly's arm.

Kelly stiffened briefly, then sighed, "Okay, I won't interfere, but I will call the credit card company and make a complaint."

"Thank you, Kelly." Molly relaxed her shoulders. "That way we can concentrate on finding Blue."

"You're right. I'm letting myself get distracted by side issues. The important thing is you have a safe place to live for now."

Kelly leaned back, "So what's the next step? I have to admit the information from head office didn't help much."

"Tom is running his sting today, that may give us something. Maybe if you can't track the corporation to the fire, we should try tracking the people; do checks on Wanda and the rest."

"We ran a basic check on all of them," Kelly rapped their knuckles on the table.

"Before, or after, we figured out it was arson?"

Kelly frowned, then sagged in their seat, "It won't hurt to run them again and it's no more useless than anything else I'm doing."

"You said the Fire Commissioner didn't find a mechanism, what does that mean?"

"Arson is usually determined because there is an accelerant or something else that doesn't belong on the scene. Even very hot fires may not burn things like one would expect. Here it's been determined the cause was a grease fire. There is nothing there that shouldn't be. Blue and I were talking about that when…" Kelly trailed off.

"Maybe we should do some research," Molly leaned back and stared at the ceiling. "Perhaps there's a firefighter who wouldn't mind playing with fire."

"It's worth trying," Kelly said, "though how it will get us closer to Blue, I don't know."

"Why would they go after Blue?" Molly drew on the table with a finger. "He's no expert. If he knew something about the fire, he would have said right away. What if they grabbed Blue to keep him away from you?"

"From me?" Kelly's eyes went wide. "I get it. If they think I'm involved with Blue. The longer I stay, the more likely I will find something. They're too smart to attack me directly."

"Who knew that you and Blue were spending time together?"

"Anybody at the motel. I ran into his room to talk with him — it was pretty obvious. The problem will be tying that knowledge to someone strong enough to consider action."

"That's why we go and burn things," Molly grinned. "Whenever Blue had a problem, he'd do something that had no relationship to the issue. He said it let his mind sort through things without him distracting it."

"And how will we convince the fire department that teaching us about grease fires is worth their time?"

"You said you weren't an expert on fires. Anyone I've met who claimed to be an expert on something couldn't stop talking about it."

***

Molly walked through the gate into what looked like a set for a post-apocalyptic movie.

"We do grease fire demonstrations on a regular basis so the setup is here," Kris waved at the concrete area with house sized blocks and a tower scattered about, then led them to one of the blocks, "Here is where we have the demonstrations. We use the barbeque so we don't need to run power. Just pretend it's a stove."

"The stove had a hood over it," Kelly walked around and examined the area.

"We can add a hood for the next shot." Kris unlocked a cabinet and hoisted out a pot to put on the stove, then filled it three-quarters full from a large pail of fry grease. Kris set a bucket into position on an arm sticking out of the wall and added water from another jug. A pin held it in place, tied to a long length of chain.

They walked farther than Molly expected before Kris told them to wait on the line painted on the concrete beside a fire extinguisher. She returned to the BBQ to light the propane, then backed away holding the chain to be sure it didn't tangle.

"Someone modified the barbeque to direct all the heat at the pot, so it doesn't take long to heat up. We never know when it will catch fire, so we make sure everyone is well out of the way before lighting the barbeque. We could rig something to set fire to the grease but the demonstration is more effective if it bursts spontaneously into flame."

When it roared into flame, Molly squeaked and jumped back. Kris didn't laugh. When Molly stood beside them again, Kris tugged on the rope tilting the bucket of water into the pot. The one metre flame shot up much higher than the top of the concrete.

"And that is why you don't throw water on a grease fire," Kris grinned at them. "It never gets old. Never, never do this at home. You can't assume you can control it. Here, it is surrounded by concrete so it can't get of control."

Kris walked forward with the fire extinguisher and used foam to put out the fire.

"While we wait for it to cool, let me show you around some more." They looked at a set up where firefighters practiced with actual flame, "We set up different scenarios for them, they get used to being around fire without losing awareness of what the flames are doing."

Back at the grease fire demo, Kris installed a fire hood over the pot. Then, he set up the demonstration again, "We are going to back up a bit more. You'll see why."

This time when she pulled the chain the column of flame hit the hood and splashed outward in all directions bouncing across the concrete.

"That explains the pattern at the apartment," Kelly sighed and rubbed the back of their neck, "but gets us no closer to how it started."

"I can't see anyone getting that close without being burned severely." Molly bit her lip, "There wasn't a bucket but there had to be water. So, what else holds water?"

"...paper cups, freezer bags, plastic bottles," Kelly listed, counting them off on their fingers.

"Balloons," Kris added. "Didn't you ever have water fights?"

"It would still be a high risk to toss a balloon close

enough to land in the pot."

"Probably wouldn't need to hit the pot — the flame would burst the balloon easily enough."

"It was a small apartment," Kelly pointed to where the grease had spattered across the concrete. "The walls and cupboards would redirect it in unpredictable ways."

"Then it has to be a system where the randomness doesn't affect the outcome," Kris shrugged and began extinguishing the flames.

***

"That was fun but what did we learn?" Molly slumped back in the booth.

Kelly sipped their coffee and tilted their head.

"Water and flaming grease are a deadly mix. The challenge is bringing them together without dying or leaving any evidence behind."

"If they set something up, then left like Kris said, it wouldn't matter when it went off as long as they were out first."

Tom slid into the booth.

"How did it go?"

"Terrifying," Molly said. "Tara was lucky to get out. I'm sure she had only seconds."

"Why Tara?" Tom asked. "We because she was a drug addict and easy to blame for the fire? But if it is supposed to be an accident that wouldn't matter."

"What if they were trying to kill Tara?" Molly dug an ice cube from her glass and pushed it around the table, "Why?"

"I would say for money," Kelly closed their eyes. "Too

many things come down to money."

"You might be interested in what I learned..." Tom leaned forward, "All the people who showed up were small contractors or did the work themselves. The process was that they did the repair and handed the invoice to someone in the building, or more exactly, put it under the door. In a day or so, they'd get an e-transfer for the amount. Then they got a notice saying the door to drop invoices under had moved next door. That new door apparently was the Abira's apartment where he and his wife died.

"So the original door was either Tara's or whover was past Abira's?" Molly frowned. "No, if all the note said was 'next door', the original had to be at the end of the hall. That would have to be Tara's."

"It would make sense if the victims were supposed to be the ones who took in the invoices. But why?" Kelly rubbed her neck.

"I'm still checking but it looks like a lot of the repairs were not the ones needed, only enough to convince the tenants." Tom spread his hands, "If they were shorting on the repairs, their liability would go up. Get rid of whoever knows that and the risk of detection goes down."

"Why now," Kelly asked, "if it had been running smoothly for so long?"

"The last unpaid invoice was for fixing a crack in the laundry room floor. The man wrote that he'd found asbestos insulation on the pipes in the boiler room, and they'd need to call in people to look at it."

"Anything about the crack between Tara's and Abira's?" Kelly crumpled their napkin into a ball.

"The building inspector wasn't impressed with the fix. Maybe the guy did it himself and submitted the bill." Kelly shrugged and flattened the napkin out before turning it into a ball again.

"Whoever set the fire knew Tara took drugs and left her balcony door open, and that Abira submitted an invoice for a crack in the fire wall. That suggests someone inside the building." Molly looked at the water on the table. "Or they were in contact with someone. Wanda did act like she knew everyone's business and it explains her saying she knew people."

"Is she the arsonist or a snitch?"

"If she knew what to do, I could believe she'd set the fire. But would she burn her own home?"

"If she was paid enough compensation," Kelly grimaced. "It is sad what humans will do for money."

"Looks like I'm paying another visit to Wanda."

"And take another beating? No way!" Kelly leaned forward.

"If she is unsure if I'm connected, I should be safe enough and this time I don't think playing weak is the plan."

"If you must, but don't go inside anywhere with her."

"Got you!" Molly nodded vigorously, "Get information — not dead."

***

It was still light out when Molly strolled down to the motel. A plywood wall replaced the caution tape. It ran half the length of the single floor building, closing off five rooms. That had to be a blow to the owner.

The other building was bigger and newer. It had rooms on both sides except for where the garbage bins and utility rooms were — where Wanda had jumped Molly.

Wanda still lived in the room at the end of the old building. The curtains were closed and the lights were on. Molly walked over and banged on the door. After a few minutes of banging Wanda opened the door, then tried to shut it but Molly had her foot in the way.

"We're going for a walk, Wanda," Molly smiled pleasantly.

"No. I'm not going with you."

"I'm not asking," Molly widened her smile. "You like playing with fire?"

Wanda looked like she'd been stabbed. Molly took her arm.

"What do you want with me?" Wanda squeaked.

"Just a friendly chat." Molly squeezed her arm again. "I've been learning a lot about fire these days."

"Your boss, who is he?"

"You know I'm not going to tell you that. I like not being dismembered and scattered for the coyotes."

Wanda glared at Molly. "Your boss gets me out; I don't care about money but I gotta be gone."

"I will take the message back." Molly patted Wanda's hand, "See, that wasn't so bad, was it?"

Wanda bolted back to her room and Molly sauntered away, waving at Harley as she passed. The dog sat by her rail like a queen overseeing her domain.

***

"Wanda." The voice on the phone made her want to puke.

Columbia Smoke

"They know about the fire," Wanda stammered.

"Who?" The word came sharp.

"I don't know, I swear. The tramp's boss."

"By tramp, you mean the girl you beat up the other day? If you are going to start something, Wanda, you should be prepared to finish it. My people will meet you on Peterson Trail under the highway. They will have your money and your ticket out of here. Better hurry — if they leave before you get there, you're on your own."

***

Blue woke to someone standing over him. A glass of rye sat beside him. He picked it up and half drained it. The person snorted and stomped out of the room, slamming the door behind him. Blue rolled over and let the whisky drain from his mouth into a crack in the floor.

Blue's mind was fuzzy, not so much from the alcohol as from fighting the desire to drink himself into oblivion. Anger saved him. It burned through his veins making him shake uncontrollably.

He had no idea what he was angry about, but it felt right. Blue picked up the bottle and staggered around pretending to drink, then leaning against the wall and spraying it out. When he tripped and landed on his back, something winked at him.

You're being watched. That's a camera.

"If there is a camera, there's a mic."

Blue dragged himself up and ranted random nonsense, working through the second bottle of rye, swallowing as little as possible. He fell against the wall and slumped to the floor, leaning forward with his hand

keeping the bottle from spilling a drop.
"What's the plan?"

Chapter 19

Saturday, June 19

Martha decided to walk with Molly to the A&W for breakfast. "I'm blind but I'm in good shape. It will be fine."

Martha put her hand on Molly's arm and followed her along the sidewalk over to the A&W.

Molly kept up a litany of description and warning. "Wonder — is this how a seeing eye dog feels but without the talking?"

The Pointy Shoes clapped in delight when Martha walked in. Gertie and Viv seated her like royalty. Bobbie went to the counter to order. Though Molly volunteered, Bobbie insisted she knew every order so it was easier.

When Simon came to give them their food, he spoke softly, "When I got up this morning, Wanda's door was wide open, and the place looked ransacked."

"She ran, but why ransack the place?" Molly picked up her hash brown and nibbled at it.

"If the door was open, the others would have gone through and taken anything of value. They are vultures," Simon went back to his work.

Guilt nagged at Molly. Wanda had run because of her. She'd pushed too hard and now they would never hear from her about the fire.

"About Molly's money, the first thing to do is talk to the manager. They may not know what is going on." Dusi dabbed at her mouth with her napkin. Her expression said she didn't believe that.

"I will do some research. There's probably a corporation behind them," Bobbie grinned and Katerine sighed.

"Last time you spent a day arguing with some lawyer."

"I won the argument, didn't I?" Bobbie sat up straight putting on a mock hurt face.

"I think she gave in out of exhaustion," Viv winked at Molly while the other ladies laughed.

"Anyone need a refill?" Simon held up the pot. As he poured, he talked to Molly, "Fran came in with her dad yesterday. He said she could see me when I could pay the rent on a decent apartment with the money I'd earned. I asked the manager for more hours. He said he didn't have any extra but I could take a second job as long as I showed up for my shifts. It's hard, this working thing, but it isn't going to kill me."

"My nephew has a landscaping business." Gertie wrote a number on a napkin. "He's always looking for people — says not enough people want to work hard these days. Tell him Aunt Gertie told you to call."

Simon took the number and went to the next table.

"It is good to be back," Martha sipped on her coffee. "Molly dear, you go with Dusi to the motel. One of the others will give me a ride home."

"Okay," Molly looked at her clothes, at least they were clean but she still bought most of her wardrobe from thrift shops.

Dusi looked at her watch, "If we get there just after nine, I think we have the best chance of talking with the manager. You explain the situation and I will jump in if I have to."

Molly swallowed hard, but nodded and followed Dusi out to a Mercedes and climbed in.

"My one indulgence," Dusi patted the steering wheel, then set the car in motion.

Dusi parked outside the office of the motel, "I need to make a call, don't mind me...I'll be keeping an eye on you."

Molly squared her shoulders, walked into the motel and waited to talk to the person at the counter. Her heart sunk as she recognized the person who had thrown her out. The person ahead of her scribbled on a piece of paper, then picked up a bag and walked out past Molly.

"What may I — " the woman recognized Molly and frowned, "What do *you* want?"

"I would like to speak to the manager."

"*I'm* the day manager; you've talked to me. Now, get out!"

"You mentioned a contract. I would like to see it. I certainly never got a copy." Molly met the woman's eyes and heat flowed from her gut into her arms and legs, "I would like to have a lawyer look at it."

The manager laughed, "Your people don't have lawyers, they have parole officers."

"Are you saying, then, that you refuse to give me a copy of a contract you say I signed?" Molly leaned forward, "I'm sure the City will be impressed. That's my next stop. Didn't they issue that business license?"

"Right! I'm scared..." The woman poked Molly in the

chest with a hard finger, "You're a tramp — garbage like the rest — who is going to believe you?"

"I do." Dusi stepped forward, "You're going to a lot of effort to avoid filling this young woman's request, and so rudely too. I don't think I will stay here after all. I couldn't take being around such awful people." Dusi swept out the door and Molly followed. She glimpsed the manager's pale face as she got into the car with Dusi. Then George stepped around a corner and glared at her with cold eyes and a slight sneer on his face.

"You were marvellous," Dusi smiled and clapped her hands. When she squeezed Molly's arm, her hand was only a little darker. She drove away from the motel, "I got much more than I'd hoped for."

"You got it?"

"While you were speaking to the manager, I was recording my to-do list for the day. It isn't my fault every word the manager said is clear as a bell too. Since you mentioned the City, let's go there next."

The next hour was a bewildering maze of offices and people who were all very sympathetic but said it wasn't their jurisdiction.

"I'm not surprised," Dusi waved Molly to a seat at Art We Are. The walls were covered with art in all kinds of styles. People sat chatting at tables and looking very relaxed. No one gave her a second glance.

"Here," Dusi put a plate with an enormous cookie on the table. "They'll bring tea in a minute."

"Sounds good."

The atmosphere helped ease the tension in her neck.

"Did you see the caretaker watching us?"

"The unpleasant looking man in the coveralls?" Dusi frowned. "Just a glimpse. He reminds me of some people at home who made less trouble than they wanted but more than they should."

The tea arrived and Molly sipped at hers. She'd grown up preferring coffee but tea was nice to chat over.

"I'm going to guess that those thieves at the motel aren't the only problem you're facing. None of us Pointy Shoes grandmothers started out wealthy and sophisticated. I was born a slave in Nigeria. Yes, there are still slaves but they called us workers and told us we had to pay them much money to be free. By the time some people came to free us and put the slavers in jail, I was as hard and cruel as a stone. I did whatever I needed to in order to survive and I refused the help offered by the people who freed me. Then I got sick. I closed my eyes thinking I would never open them again."

Dusi broke off a bit of the cookie and chewed thoughtfully.

"I woke up in a white room in a hospital run by the same people who freed me. A woman came to visit. She told me, 'Leave if you want: stay if you want. Help forced is only another kind of tyranny.'"

"She sounds like Blue," Molly fought back tears. "He told me I had to make my own choices, then he backed me completely when I did."

"Yes, it is hard to allow others to make what you think is the wrong choice. My daughter struggled to allow her son to travel here to study." Dusi sighed. "The people from the hospital put me in school and told me to learn what I wanted. The desire to learn became a raging fire. I finished school, got a scholarship to university, and ended up becoming a lawyer to fight for people to have the right to make wrong choices. Many 'business people' who relied on slaves, hated me over the years but it didn't slow my passion. Then, a younger generation took up the fight and I thought I'd retire. My husband died many years ago and I didn't want to live with my daughter and look over her shoulder. So, I came here and never once have I regretted it."

Molly's phone rang before she could reply.

"Sorry, I need to answer this. Hello, Kelly."

"Molly, I just saw the news. Wanda was found near Peterson Creek. The report was lacking in detail but it was definitely murder."

"Simon said her door was open..." Molly dropped her phone and ran to the back, hoping the washroom was there. She barely made it before her breakfast came up. Her t-shirt was drenched. She stripped it off and buried it in the trash before the smell made her puke again. Then she used paper towels to try to clean up the mess.

Someone knocked on the door.

"Miss, are you all right? Your friend is worried about you."

"Yes! No!" Molly sobbed, "Could you ask her to come here?"

The door clicked open and Dusi slipped in, it felt like when her grandmother came to help her when she was sick in Calgary.

"Oh dear!" She wet a paper towel and cleaned Molly's face and chest, "You can't go out like that. Give me a minute."

Molly didn't want to let her go but Dusi had slipped out before she could protest. Her jeans, too, were a mess. She took them off and stuffed them into the garbage, wiped herself with more paper towels, then huddled in a corner away from the mess.

"I'm coming back in." Dusi slipped in and handed Molly a dress, "Put this on and see if it fits."

The dress was a rainbow of colours, it fit comfortably, dropping past her knees.

"The staff said they would clean up and not to worry about it. Things like this happen." Dusi pulled Molly out of the bathroom and they returned to the table. The server came over with a cup of tea.

"It's ginger, sip it slowly and it will settle your stomach. Your friend told us you got some bad news. We're so sorry."

"When you dashed off, your friend on the phone was concerned. I suggested she meet us here."

A few minutes later Kelly and Tom came in.

"I'm glad you're all right." Kelly sat while Tom went to the counter, "It has to be a shock after talking to her last night."

"Wanda knew about the fire — said she'd talk to me if I got her out of town. I was a terrible person. What if she went and killed herself?"

"She didn't kill herself," Tom sat down. "I called and told them it might affect our investigation. The officer didn't tell me much but said they were treating it as murder and could I come in and talk with them, sooner rather than later."

"I'll go with you," Molly said.

"I'm not sure that's a good idea."

"I want to ask them about Blue."

"Okay then," Tom shook his head. "Don't go volunteering any information.

Molly finished her tea as Kelly and Dusi chatted in a way Molly could never make work.

"I am glad you are helping Molly deal with the motel, looks like you have a better handle on it than I would have."

"It comes from getting old and not being in a hurry," Dusi chuckled. "I've found very few things that demand an instant response: fire, flood, blood."

Molly followed Tom out of the café, leaving Dusi and Kelly still talking. They walked along Victoria.

"I've never spent much time in this part of the city." Molly shook her head, "Didn't know what I was missing."

"Life can be like that — we get too busy surviving to live."

At Sixth Street, they turned to walk up to Battle Street.

"Can't say that visiting a police station is high on my to-do list!" Molly wrapped her arms around herself.

"You going to be okay?"

"Don't have a choice. I need to find out where Blue is." Molly pushed the door open and led the way in.

"Hello," Tom talked to a woman through a heavy sheet of glass, "It seems that my insurance investigation may intersect with a woman's body found this morning." He passed a card through the slot.

"Take a seat and someone will be out."

There wasn't much to see; a few chairs in an L-shaped space. The only reading was posters and pamphlets. Molly looked at the wanted posters but they were dull — nothing like the movies.

"Tom?" A big police officer came around the corner. He stopped and frowned at Molly, "You left the motel."

"They kicked me out," she said as she pointed at her face, "They don't like my kind of people."

"We were looking for you.'

"I assure you, Constable, I was not deliberately hiding. Surviving the last few days has been as much as I can handle."

"Come with me," he walked away. Tom looked at Molly and she shrugged.

Constable Post led them to an interview room. It didn't look at all like it did on TV, except for the video camera in the corner.

"Sit down," Constable Post started the video camera. "Constable Post interviewing Molly Callister, June 19" with Tom…"

"Hintle," Tom frowned. "Should Molly have a lawyer?"

"If she feels she needs one at any point, she can ask for one. She's not being charged or detained."

"Fine, let's get this done," Molly swallowed.

"Would you like some water?"

"Sure," Molly accepted the bottle from the constable

and opened it. It gave her hands something to do.

"Witnesses say you had an argument with the victim early yesterday evening."

"I wouldn't call it an argument. We walked around and I suggested Wanda knew something about the apartment fire and Blue's disappearance."

"You pulled the victim from her apartment."

"I wasn't going to go in, not after she kicked the shit out of me before."

"Nothing was reported."

"That's right."

"So, I just have your word for it."

Molly pointed to her cheek, "There's a bit of bruising still there. Also, Simon, don't know his last name but he lives in the same motel, helped me after."

"You threatened her with your suggestions?"

"You'd probably call it that. I implied that the people she thought I worked for were annoyed by her."

"Explain a bit clearer..."

"Wanda beat me up because she didn't like seeing me around the motel. After, she told me she knew people who could make me disappear like Blue. I heard a black van took him. Wanda wanted to be important and bragged. I grew up with that kind of people. The last thing you'd do is brag about it. I played her assumptions to scare her."

"Just for the record, did you have anything to do with her death?"

"No. She was a bitch but that doesn't deserve death. I wanted the information she had — won't get that from a dead person."

"Perhaps your questioning got out of hand."

"I know, and you should know, that beating someone will get you blood, but no truth. She wanted out and I offered her an 'out' if she talked."

"You were lying to her."

"I thought I was, but if she'd come to talk, I think I would have given her some money and a ticket out of town. She was in over her head and falling apart."

"You were involved in a drug case last year."

"If you call being abducted and forced at gunpoint to pack drugs, then locked in a box to be sold to someone in Vancouver, then, yes. If you want more information, ask Constable Madoc, and tell her hello for me."

"I did speak to her," Constable Post said and put the paper in a folder. "She said you were tough as nails and got yourself off the street."

"Blue got me off the street. Without him I'd be on a corner in Vancouver, or more likely, dead."

"Threatening people is not a good idea."

"You're right. I feel sick about it now," Molly drew in a shuddering breath and took a long drink from the bottle.

"That will do for now," Constable Post said. "You can wait in the front until I'm done with Mr. Hintle."

"Okay," Molly followed the big cop to the door and went back to the waiting room.

Chapter 20

After saying farewell to Dusi, Kelly returned to their hotel room and booted up their computer. It would distract them from what was going on.

They signed on to their account and on impulse checked the ownership of the motel which had taken Molly's money. The Pointy Shoes — Kelly smiled at the name — were checking through their channels to see what chain franchised the place. The ownership was more complex than they'd expected. *"Was an out-of-country owner trying to avoid taxes?"* They followed the tracks of who owned what until they arrived at a page which sent a chill down their back. A corporation number which looked familiar; the first half of the number contained their private cell number. It wasn't the first time they'd come upon that company.

Kelly pulled up her research on the apartment building. There it was, the same shell corporation. They started a new search with the shell corporation as the centre and tracked what it owned. A few times it again crossed over with the apartment search.

They lost track of time and jumped when someone knocked on the door.

"Hey, it's almost suppertime," Tom grinned at them. "The police station was nothing to worry about. The cop was more interested in Molly than what I'm doing. She did great, gave honest answers and little for him to get a grip on. Apparently, she's impressed the hell out of another cop in the area and that is keeping him from doing too much fishing. Security's report on Molly's visit matched hers. They didn't see anybody obviously watching."

"Catching killers is not our job," Kelly winced at how it came out.

"I know," Tom said. "There are all kinds of brewpubs in the area. I thought we could try another one out."

"Give me thirty minutes," Kelly shook the cobwebs from their head.

***

The Redbeard was busy but they got a table on the patio and watched the foot traffic on Tranquille. Kelly savoured the very nice stout while Tom sipped on something named 'Swamp Donkey'.

A shoving match began across the street and Kelly waited for the sirens as someone stood in their doorway with a phone to their ear.

Instead, a few minutes later, two women in blue vests showed up and looked like they knew the men. They kept their distance but whatever they were saying must have got through, as the combatants separated and looked a bit sheepish.

After a bit more talk, the pair walked away in the opposite direction. The women said hello to the person in the doorway, then strolled along, chatting with a woman pushing a shopping cart.

Their meals arrived and Kelly gave her attention to the very interesting meal in front of them. There was no need to rush. One of the few things Tom had put his foot down about, mealtimes they relaxed. It had yet to cause a problem with their work.

***

Molly wasn't used to wearing a dress. Jeans and t-shirt or blouse were her uniform, though her grandmother had bought her non-denim pants she liked.

People looked at her differently — she couldn't quite define the difference. The breezed tugged at the skirt. The tiny purse she carried didn't match the dress but when she looked at purses and shoes in one of the stores, the prices made her cringe. That was a week's wages at her job in Alberta.

Molly climbed up to Seymour and discovered a farmers' market. The vendors looked like they were ready to pack up, so Molly decided she'd come back next week. While she was downtown, she might as well explore a bit. Martha made it clear that Molly did not need to stay at the house all the time.

Seymour had a very different feel from Victoria but it also had thrift shops. Molly wandered through them. She considered getting sandals but they wouldn't be good with all the walking she did.

Up at Columbia, Molly sat in a park and watched families play. Children ran through the grass and mobbed the amazing playground equipment. The air filled with squeals and laughter. Parents watched or chatted with other parents.

"This is how it should be." She sat on a bench to take it in.

A young girl, no more than eight or nine, ran up to her.

"I like your dress," She spun in a circle, "You like mine?"

"It looks good on you," Molly smiled.

"Yours is nicer; it makes your skin shine. You Shuswap? I am." She put her arm against Molly's and it matched exactly.

"Ciara, don't be bothering people," a woman who looked to be Ciara's grandmother sauntered over.

"It's alright." Molly reached out to shake hands, "I'm Molly."

"Hanna," her grip was firm and warm, "Have I seen you before?" The grandmother peered at Molly, her forehead wrinkled in thought.

"I wouldn't think so. I just got back in town this week from school in Alberta."

"What were you studying?" Hanna tugged on Ciara's braid and the girl giggled.

"Getting ready for university — I'm taking social work at TRU."

"The band has funds to help students if they need it."

"I'm not registered," Molly snapped out the words and immediately regretted it. "Sorry, it's not your fault." Guilt made her want to explain more, "I was abandoned as an infant and grew up in the foster care system."

She sealed her lips before she got to being a hooker and addict but a cloud over Hanna's face made her wonder if the woman guessed.

"It makes me sad how many of our people are growing up without knowing their heritage."

"I'm staying with Gramma in the motel. We got

evicted 'cause of the fire," the girl bounced on her toes.

"Evacuated, Ciara," Hanna laughed. "A fire is threatening the east end of the reserve."

"The fire people are trying to save the eagles. I like the eagles. There's no school while we're evacuated. I like school. We get to sing at school," Ciara announced. "You want to hear?"

Without waiting for an answer, she straightened and music erupted from her. People in the park looked over, then went back to what they were doing. It was probably Molly's imagination but the noise in the background seemed quieter. Ciara moved from what had to be a Shuswap song, to a piece off the radio.

"Ciara would sing all day." Hanna sat down beside Molly. "Has since she could make sounds."

"She has a beautiful voice," Molly kept her voice low so she could hear the song.

"Poor girl wants voice lessons. She sees them on YouTube and tries to copy them but it's hard without a teacher."

"That's too bad," Molly clapped as Ciara finished her song and started another. This one somehow blended the traditional sounding music with the modern.

"What songs do you like singing?" Ciara came over and pulled on Molly's hand. "I'll sing them with you."

"I don't know if I can sing," Molly stopped herself from pulling her hand free.

"I'll teach you," Ciara pulled harder.

"Ciara, leave Molly alone, not everyone wants to sing all the time."

"She didn't say she didn't want to, but she didn't know how."

Molly gave in and let Ciara pull her up while Hanna shook her head.

"You must stand straight but not stiff," Ciara's tone shifted, and Molly smiled. *Must be from the videos.*

"Like this?" Molly tried to copy Ciara's stance from earlier.

"Close," the girl moved Molly until she was satisfied. "Now you have to breathe all the way down to your tummy." She inhaled slowly and Molly wondered where all the air was fitting. Trying to match the girl, she ran out of space much sooner.

"Breathe in and push against my hand." They continued with Ciara talking constantly until she stepped back, "Now, sing a note."

"What note?" Molly asked.

"The one in here," Ciara tapped Molly's temple.

Molly closed her eyes and listened for a note. She hummed it, then opened her mouth trying to remember everything Ciara had told her. What came out wasn't nearly as clear as the girl's but Ciara clapped her hands. They practiced a while longer until Hanna clapped her hands.

"That's enough for now. You have to get home to practice." Hanna stood, "Say thank you to Molly."

"Thanks, Molly. I'm singing at the Indigenous Day celebration at the pow wow grounds. You want to come and hear me?"

"That's Monday. She's on in the morning." Hanna added.

"I will do my best," Molly made a note on her phone.

"Okay." Ciara beamed at Molly. "Promise?" She held out her hand.

"I can't promise to be there, but I promise to try very hard," Molly took Ciara's hand.

"What are these?" Ciara pointed to Molly's scars from years of addiction.

"Ciara!" Hanna said sharply.

"Those are my battle scars," Molly crouched to talk to the girl, "I had to fight for my life, and these remind me I won."

"Wow!" Ciara's eyes widened. "Bye!" She ran over to Hanna who wiped her eyes but smiled at Molly. They walked away across the park.

Maybe one of the ladies would drive Molly, she wasn't even sure where the pow wow grounds were. She started up Columbia thinking about Ciara. *Must be nice to know where you come from.*

As she passed the hospital, the hill grew steep. Molly used the railing to pull herself up, stopping now and again to see the view. The hill down to the houses was steep but a few trails ran up and down. At the top of the rail a deer lifted its head to stare at her

The traffic on the hill was light and the deer ignored the occasional passing car.

It startled and vanished in a bound. Molly looked behind her as two men jumped out of a big SUV.

The first one reached her and the drills from Judo kicked in. She lowered her center of gravity and pulled the man forward to unbalance him. She pivoted and used his momentum and her hip to throw him. The man rolled under the railing and down the hill, swearing furiously.

"Baby, a little kung fu shit isn't going to save you." A door on the other side of the black vehicle opened and the second man grinned.

The blare of a horn interrupted them. The man jumped in the open doors and the SUV squealed its tires as it took off turning off Columbia to vanish in a subdivision.

Molly looked around. An old man was leaning toward her from the driver's seat of a red Mustang but she couldn't hear him over the pounding of her heart.

On the other side of the road, a man jogged across toward her. Molly panicked and sprinted away up the hill. Her already-tired legs complained, but all she could think of was to get as far away as possible. She glanced back to see the two talking and pointing toward her.

She sprinted across the road and a couple drivers honked their horns at her. Pushing herself up the hill, Molly tried to think of what to do. Rod was walking Harley away from the outlook — Harley would protect her, but Rod didn't like her. She pushed, dodging through the line of people getting on the bus. A few shouted at her but Molly couldn't stop her flight. Starbucks beckoned to her at the McGill intersection.

Molly burst through the door, gasping for breath. The people in the shop stared at her but the man behind the counter came around and guided her to a room in the back. He handed her a glass of water and made a motion for her to stay put. When the door closed behind him, she was alone.

No sound came through the door and as her heart retuned to its normal rhythm, Molly wondered how she'd explain the situation. Her phone rang and she almost jumped out of her skin.

"Molly, dear, I was getting something out of the freezer to heat up. If you're going to be home soon, I'll take one out for you too."

"Martha, could you call one of the ladies and ask them to pick me up. I'm in the Starbucks at McGill and Columbia. Tell them to ask for pointy shoes."

"Are you all right?"

"I am now, but I need your help."

"Katerine is here — she's on her way." Martha hung up.

The door opened and a woman came in. Her name tag said 'Rita'

"We don't see anything suspicious but you're welcome to stay in the staff room a bit longer."

"I've called a friend to come pick me up. She'll be an older lady and she'll ask for pointy shoes."

Rita looked at her for a long moment, then nodded, "I'll come get you when they arrive."

***

"Molly!" The name came to Blue and woke him up. He sat up and fought the blur of the alcohol in his brain. Even if he spat most of it out or poured it through a crack in the floor, the rye had its claws into him. A face appeared in his mind: black hair, dusky skin, and brown eyes that could be soft or hard as stones.

There was something about her he had to remember. The idea that she was in danger made him pace the floor. The reek of smoke only made him more nervous. It was getting worse, sending him into coughing fits. Blue threw the bottle to smash against the wall.

Good idea, but you'll want to aim at their eye. Blue's gaze went to where he'd seen a glint reflected from the ceiling. He wanted to smash it right away but his eyes burned, and he closed them to get relief from the smoke.

Chapter 21

Sunday, June 20

Molly did laundry and hung up her dress in the closet. She rearranged the stuff in her room. Then she walked through the house trying to memorize where everything was placed.

Once in a while, she'd go and open the front door and her heart would race until she felt dizzy.

What's going on? I really was abducted and I didn't act like this.

"What's wrong, dear? You're very restless this morning."

"Yesterday shook me up worse than I thought," Molly closed the door yet again.

"Why don't you call your friends? You don't have to fight these things on your own. For decades after the war, I bought too much food. My husband teased me that we could live for a year on what I had stashed away," Martha smiled. "He might have been right. After a while, when I didn't starve, I was able to cut back. Yet, if you look through my cupboards, you'll still find more food than is reasonable for one old lady."

"Right! But I've been grabbed more than once and I didn't get the heebie jeebies like this."

"What was different about those times?" Martha headed for the kitchen, "I'll put some tea on, and we can talk about it."

Molly followed, bemused at this old woman who didn't bat an eye at the idea this wasn't the first time Molly'd been grabbed off the street.

Martha unerringly moved through the kitchen and soon the tea pot sat under its chicken cover and Molly nibbled on a cookie.

"Tell me about these other times," Martha settled herself in her chair and faced Molly's direction.

Molly recounted her experiences with Tad last year. Had it only been a year? She felt like she might have been talking about someone other than herself.

"My!" Martha poured tea into the delicate cups, "All the most interesting people I know have had rough times and have done things they regret. None of the Pointy Shoes have had an easy life, though it's hard to tell now."

"I see people going about their lives and I have a hard time imagining myself like that but a lot of them have stories too," Molly sipped at the tea.

"As long as we're prepared to listen to their stories, we'll be able to help. If we don't listen, then all we're doing is another kind of abuse no matter how pure our motives."

"That's what Blue does with the Peer Ambassadors. He said once that it was listening until the people recovered themselves."

"Sounds like an important job." Martha picked up a cookie and bit into it. "Going back to your story, the difference I see is in the early occasions; you knew the person. You knew it would be bad but you could predict what kind of bad."

"That's true enough," Molly pushed the heels of her

hands against her eyes. "It was pretty random. I'm looking at a deer; then people are jumping me."

"I'm sure the deer was as startled as you," Martha chuckled.

"It booked it out of there fast enough," Molly took a bite and chewed on her cookie, "I said it was random but there had to be a reason. Either something to do with Wanda or the motel."

"The motel?" Marsha raised an eyebrow.

"The caretaker gives me the creeps. I thought he was just a wannabe but even wannabes can be dangerous. Maybe they saw me and the empty street and made a snap decision. Pretty ballsy to try a snatch in daylight on a busy street."

"It does have the feel of desperation," Martha drank from her cup as if they were discussing gardening, not abduction.

"Maybe the plan is not to hide myself away but to be out to draw them in, at least we'd know who it is. I'd need someone watching my back," Molly scratched her head, then sat back, "After we've finished our tea, I need to make a call."

***

Kelly drank her cold coffee without taking their eyes from the screen. Whoever set up this chain knew their stuff but Kelly was no slouch either.

The apartment building had been purchased after the motel but there was no connection between them aside from the one shared corporation.

A knock on the door and Tom carried in a fresh

coffee.

"I shudder to imagine you drinking cold coffee," he said, placing it safely to the side of the laptop and whisked the other one away.

"The apartment building is guarded and there is too much activity around the motel. If 'whoever' owns two buildings, who's to say there aren't three?"

"It would be convenient," Tom took a seat out of Kelly's line of vision. "What's the plan, boss?"

"I'm not moving from this seat until I have something useful."

Kelly's phone buzzed.

"Hello? Oh, hi Molly." They moved away from the computer and picked up the new coffee. "That's an interesting thought. I'll hand you to Tom and the two of you can plot."

Kelly was already buried deep in her search before the door closed behind Tom.

***

Molly watched Tom pull up in front of the house and before she could second guess herself, ran out to the car and jumped in.

"Let's go before I lose my nerve," Molly twisted her fingers together. *Either you slow down or quit.* She told her heart. It begrudgingly slowed and she leaned against the back of the seat.

"You good?"

"Good enough," Molly laughed. 'Don't want to be too confident."

"At this point, I'm not sure if we're talking confidence

or sanity," Tom turned onto Hillside and wound up toward the mall. At least, Molly guessed that was where he was heading. She still had only vague ideas of the area, even after studying her map app on the laptop.

They parked near the doors and Tom led them in. Then, he checked the map before heading deeper in. They arrived at the food court and he bought a burger. Molly's heart might have been cooperating but her stomach refused the idea of eating.

She bought a drink just to have something in front of her.

Tom ate his burger in a leisurely fashion.

"Relax." He put the garbage on the tray. "We're meeting friends of mine."

Molly looked around but didn't see anyone she could imagine as Tom's friend.

"You're clear." A man said as he sat down. Molly jumped up and almost bolted but caught herself.

"I'll get rid of the garbage," she offered, and was surprised at how normal she sounded by the time she retook her seat; Molly had cajoled her brain into working.

"This is Jack. He's a contract security specialist with our company."

"Of course." Molly sighed and picked up her drink to take a sip, "You've filled him in?"

"He did." Jack looked nothing like a security specialist; balding under his ballcap and no bulging muscles, "I would normally refuse anything like this plan. We aren't in the movies!"

"No rocket launchers?" Molly grinned.

"They attract attention," Jack's lips twitched. "Here's the deal. Tom filled me in, and we can make this work if you play it my way."

"You're the specialist." Molly leaned forward "So tell me the rules.

***

Molly perched on the rail of the outlook. She had a sketchbook and pencils but insisted she buy a bag to carry them. She'd found one in Value Village that was gloriously beaten up. Now it leaned against her leg.

Smoke dimmed the view, smudging the details. Molly lost herself in the challenge of sketching the smoky air. A cold nose bumped her hand. A big black dog looked up at her.

"I'm not supposed to touch you. Sorry, girl."

"Do you believe the world is a good place?" Rod stood behind her and a chill ran down her spine. But she didn't feel his anger this time.

"I don't think it is a bad place," Molly said slowly. "We make it into what we make it."

"Not everyone gets a choice." Rod pointed over her shoulder across to the confluence of the North and South Thompson, "On the other side of that mountain, a fire is burning. People were ordered to leave."

"As long they are alive, they can rebuild."

"Rebuild!" Rod's hand dropped on her shoulder. "When I was child, men came to my village. They put a knife in my hand and a gun against my sister's head. 'Choose,' they said. 'Kill your father or let your sister die'."

"That's horrible," Molly's hand clenched on her pencil.

"My father stepped up and asked me to kill him — helped me guide the knife. Then men shot my sister and anyone else they didn't think useful. They taught me there is no hope: no morality; only survival. When their war was lost, they turned me loose along with the other children they'd crafted into killers."

"God! That's awful."

"Hope doesn't exist," Rod squeezed her shoulder until the bones ground together, "Remember that." He walked away, Harley gave her a final lick and followed him.

Molly wiped away her tears and when she could see went back to her drawing. Blue had taught her hope.

***

No one else approached her through the afternoon. At three, she put her sketching materials away and walked back toward her new home.

The fight to keep from looking behind her made her neck and shoulders tense, until she had an horrific headache. Each black car in the corner of her eyes became a spike of pain in her temples.

The other people on the sidewalk looked at her with worry or disgust in their eyes. Some muttered epithets in stage whispers. She wanted to scream at them but that would only confirm their prejudice.

After she made it home, Molly went and collapsed on her bed.

"Molly!" Martha spoke from the door, "Are you all right? Is there anything I can get for you?"

"Thanks, but I just need to rest," Molly closed her eyes.

***

Kelly sat up and went back to her computer. They'd switched from coffee to water hours ago.

They'd found another property in the area owned by the same group of corporations. Of course, it couldn't be anything as simple as a street address. Kelly now had to work through the Property Identification to get something like a physical location.

Her phone buzzed.

"Kelly here."

"Hi, didn't see anything at the outlook or on the way home. Jack's keeping an eye on the house."

"It was a stretch from the beginning," Kelly said. "I have a bit more to report on my end. I've found something but have no idea how to get there yet."

"It's something anyway. Molly invited us to join her at a celebration of Indigenous Day at the pow wow ground tomorrow morning. Some of the Pointy Shoes may come as well."

"Sounds like fun. Maybe we need a break to get a better grip on things."

***

"Boss! That fire's getting close — we gotta book it."

"Clean up. That needs to be an empty house.'

"Got it. What about the guy?"

"What about him? Let him burn — we spent enough time on him."

Chapter 22

Monday, June 21

Blue hardly bothered to fake drinking. The smoke in the shed was thick enough to make him cough constantly. Nobody had showed up to check on him last night, nor this morning. The fires must be close and they'd abandoned him. No time to get ansty about it.

Time to get to work. Blue broke a bottle and used the sharp piece of the neck to dig at the ceiling. Everywhere else the wood was thick and heavy, but the ceiling was light tongue and groove.

The hardest work was making a hole for his fingers. After that, it was just a matter of hanging with his full weight to break the boards.

Blue gripped the rafter and used his feet on the wall to help lift him into the attic. It felt like an oven. He felt along the underside of the roof for soft spots but only stabbed his finger on nails. At the end of the shed, a big grate let smoke pour into the attic. Two good kicks knocked the grate loose. Seconds later, he dropped to the ground.

The roar was deafening — the fire had to be very close. With no other choice, Blue ran away from the fire while tearing a piece off his shirt to put over his mouth. The forest was treacherous, between roots and rocks at his feet, and the smoke obscuring his vision.

Faster than he expected, Blue burst out onto a road but red glowed through the smoke in either direction. He ran across and into the forest on the other side, immediately hitting a steep hill. Just as he was about ready to turn around, the ground levelled to a bearable incline and the forest opened up. He followed the clear patches until he stumbled on another road, though this was little more than a track through the field.

It led him to a cluster of buildings. Blue ran to the hose hanging on the wall of one and drenched himself in water, then drank as much has he could hold. He staggered out onto the road, and kept moving away from the fire.

His only goal was to put one foot in front of another.

***

Molly put on the colourful dress, though it still felt odd. At least Ciara would be able to recognize it from the stage. Molly didn't want to disappoint the girl. She was curious about the celebrations. She never thought about any heritage of her own, aside from not being registered First Nations. Maybe the time had come to get past that.

"Your step is lighter than yesterday," Martha poured a cup of tea and set it in front of Molly.

"You don't need to treat me as a guest," Molly protested.

"Which would you rather have staying with you: a guest, or someone who is only there to allow you stay at home?"

"Right. But only if you let me do some of the work."

"That sounds fair."

They ate their breakfast and Molly washed the few dishes.

"Dusi and Bobbie are here," Martha came into the

kitchen, "Leave that now and have a good time."

Molly grabbed her purse and loped out to the car.

"I was hoping for one day that it didn't feel like I was living in a smoker." Molly climbed in and did up her seatbelt.

"The fire by Paul Lake is getting worse," Bobbie said. "That whole area was evacuated yesterday. A lot of people are going to lose their homes."

"That's terrible!"

"It's happening more often," Bobbie backed out of the driveway. "We'll meet Kelly at her hotel. Then Dusi can ride with them to give directions.

***

There was a large circular building enclosing a grass field at the powwow grounds. It was already crowded with people wearing colourful clothing. Some were dancing to the drumming and singing. Molly walked about in a daze.

The rhythms tugged at her heart, and her feet wanted her to move. Molly headed toward where someone appeared to be announcing events.

Young people drummed and sang while others danced. All of them looked to be having fun. Ciara, visibly nervous, stepped up to the mic. Molly made her way to the front and waved. Ciara smiled and started with a traditional song. It didn't matter to Molly that she couldn't understand the words, the music held her mesmerized. Ciara sang the one she had sung at the park that mixed old with the new.

Molly stood mesmerized after Ciara left the stage.

"You all right?" Ciara tugged at Molly's hand, "Come with me." She wound through the crowd until it thinned and they walked out onto a field outside the round building.

"Molly, what's wrong? Didn't you like the song?" Ciara stared up at her worried, "Are you going to go to rehab, like Mom?"

"I'm fine," Molly said, though tears still ran down her cheeks.

"No, you aren't!" Ciara stomped her foot.

"Do you know how lucky you are to know where you came from? You have your own music and traditions. All I have is…" Molly hugged herself to hide the scars on her arms.

"Everyone comes from somewhere," Ciara frowned at her.

"I was left at a police station — like someone's lost luggage. I don't even know what name my mother would have given me."

Ciara wrapped her arms around Molly, "This is what grandmother does when I get upset. She tells me I am loved: I have a place in the world even when it doesn't feel like it. Mom loves me but she's fighting a bad monster," Ciara began to sniffle. Molly held her tight and stopped trying to understand. Slowly, the storm of emotion passed.

"Thank you, Ciara, you don't know how much this means to me. I wish I was your big sister. I'd brag about you all the time."

"You're too old to be my sister. You're like mom's age so you can be my auntie."

Next thing Molly knew, Ciara was dragging her through the crowd again.

"There they are," Ciara stopped in the middle of a group of people. Hanna raised her eyebrows.

"Where did you get off to?"

"I wanted to get an autograph from my favourite niece," a man a bit younger than Blue said, and picked up Ciara to swing her around.

"I've told you, no autographs until I have a CD." Ciara giggled, then she grabbed Molly's hand. "Listen! Molly doesn't have a family so I told her she could be part of ours."

Molly's mouth dropped open but nobody looked upset.

"Welcome, I guess," a woman said, and smiled at her. "Nobody's ever successfully changed Ciara's mind once she made a decision. I'm Vickie, and the fan here is my husband Ben…"

The names came faster than Molly could remember. There were three aunts and two uncles. A few Molly couldn't tell if they were older grandchildren or younger children of Hanna's.

"Ah Molly, there you are!" Bobbie stepped out of the crowd and the atmosphere around Molly chilled.

"Hello, Roberta," Hanna put Ciara behind her.

"Hello, Hanna," Bobbie looked around and sighed, "You know, you were right back then. The whole time, you were right. I wish I'd had the wisdom to listen to you."

"That's not going to put our families back together is it?"

"No, it won't. I'm glad Molly found you. I can't imagine a better person to be her mentor." Bobbie let her head drop, "I will leave you to your gathering. Oh, one more thing. There is a music professor at TRU who is putting together a children's choir. Applications for auditions are open until the end of the month."

"And you will drop a word in his ear?" Hanna's voice came out colder, if that was possible.

"No, he hates me almost as much as you do and with as much cause." Bobbie nodded at Molly, "Phone if you need a ride home." She turned and vanished into the crowd.

"The poor woman," Hanna said. "For twenty years she's been apologizing for her mistakes. I might forgive her if anything had changed since her day."

"Let's go back to the house and eat," Vickie said.

***

Kelly wandered through the crowd, taking in the sights. Molly had vanished but Bobbie told them she was as safe as she could be anywhere. Work kept them from events like this.

"I need a life away from work."

They would enjoy the moment. Something Kelly had never been good at.

"I like the feel of this place," Tom said. "Look at the kids running around! Not a helicopter parent in sight."

"You're right." Kelly closed their eyes and listened. "Let's be sure to enjoy ourselves."

The time passed by watching dancers and listening to singers. Off in one corner, there was a horde of children from toddlers to teens enjoying what looked like a free-for-all water balloon fight. The goal appeared to be to get as wet as possible, while soaking everyone else.

One teen held her balloon over a younger girl and popped it. They both squealed as water splashed all over them.

"Of course!" Kelly stared at the balloons, "That's it!" They pulled out their phone, then put it away. "It will wait. The office will be closed by now."

***

Blue followed the road because he had nothing else. The smoke teased him with glimpses of slopes to either side of him.

At first, Blue feared the light ahead was more fire, but it didn't look quite right — too tame. His feet wouldn't stop anyway.

As he got closer, the light resolved into a barrier with flashing lights. A vehicle parked on the other side formed a block in the smoke.

Blue couldn't be sure but there might be the silhouette of a person behind the front window. He stumbled past the barrier and headed toward the truck.

"Holy shit!" A man jumped out of the truck and ran to Blue. "Where did you come from?"

Blue tried to answer but a coughing fit hit him.

"Hang on, keep breathing!" The man guided Blue to the truck and helped him into the seat. Cool air flowed into Blue's lungs.

The man talked urgently into a radio but Blue was content to just breathe.

Chapter 23

Tuesday, June 22

Molly woke choking, with tears in her eyes. The only thing she could remember from the dream was Blue being lost in smoke, with fire all around him.

Even after she woke, smoke filled Molly's nose. She had a shower to wash the remnants of the dream out of her head.

The huge towel was the softest Molly'd ever used. *"I could get used to this!"* She shook her head. As soon as they found Blue, they'd be back to living in a little apartment. Becoming accustomed to this luxury would be foolish.

She put on her jeans and t-shirt. The dress was growing more natural but it didn't fit like a second skin. Molly wanted the reminder of where she came from, even if she wasn't sure where that was.

Her phone buzzed.

"Hi, Kelly."

"You up for breakfast and plotting?" Kelly sounded excited.

"Sounds like fun."

"We'll be there in twenty." Kelly disconnected.

Something's changed, Molly grinned.

Her phoned buzzed again.

"Hello."

"Am I speaking to Molly Callister?"

"That's me."

"Constable Post here. A John Doe was brought into the hospital yesterday. I would like you to come and see if he's your Blue."

"He's dead?" Molly's voice cracked.

"He's alive but unconscious," Constable Post said. "If you're willing, I will swing by and pick you up. I'll be there in five minutes as long as you haven't moved again."

"I haven't."

"Good."

Molly phoned Kelly and got her answering service.

"Kelly, sorry. I'll meet you at the hospital." Molly disconnected the phone and ran to the kitchen. "Martha, when Kelly and Tom get here, please let them know I've gone to the hospital."

"I will, are you okay?"

"I have no idea." Molly went outside as a police car pulled up.

The constable opened the door for her. She buckled the seatbelt with trembling hands.

The officer didn't say anything as they drove to the hospital. He parked in the reserved spot and then led Molly in through the Emergency entrance.

"Wait here for a moment," he said, and went to the admitting office to talk to the woman at the computer for a minute. She pointed down the hall and he nodded.

Molly followed him down the hall to the ICU. Her stomach hurt and the shaking grew worse.

"Here, do you want me to come in with you?"

"Let me see him first," Molly scrubbed at her eyes. The constable handed her a tissue.

"Tell them you're here to see John Doe."

Molly pushed through the door and a nurse waved her over. She explained why she was there, and the nurse guided her to a bed. The only sign of life was the monitors beeping.

"Blue!" Molly knelt beside the bed and took his hand, "Is he going to be okay?" The words came out as half-sobs.

"We're treating him for smoke inhalation but he is also exhausted. It's easier for him to sleep for now. The damage to his airways is moderate but his blood oxygen levels are good."

"You can let the officer know he can come in," Molly didn't look up, her full attention on Blue's face.

"This is your Blue then?" Constable Post had his notebook out.

"Yes," Molly forced back her sobbing, "What did they do to him?"

"When he was brought in there was alcohol in his system but more interesting was the presence of GHB which affects memory. I asked for a hair test. It will tell us what was going on before he disappeared."

"So he won't remember me when he wakes up?"

"Short term memory loss; he'll remember you but not much of the past few days." Constable Post put his notebook away. "Please don't talk to him about what happened. His statement will be confused enough without you putting ideas in his head."

"I wouldn't do—." Molly glared up at him.

"It isn't what you would intend, but what happens," the constable had no give in his expression. "Nothing about anything after he disappeared. If he asks, tell him some jerk of a cop said you weren't allowed."

***

Kelly and Tom arrived an hour after Constable Post left.

"My God!" Kelly put a hand on Molly's shoulder. "They gave us only a few minutes to talk to you unless you come out to the waiting room.

Molly had no strength to move. A nurse had put her in a chair, but she couldn't imagine standing.

"It's okay," Kelly squeezed her shoulder, "I wanted to bring you up-to-date. Tom and I figured out the mechanism for the arson. They hung a water balloon from the stove hood. The flames burst the ballon, then burned away everything. The company has asked the Fire Commissioner's office and the police to investigate."

"That's great!" Molly looked up and tried to smile.

"Is it?" Kelly's cheeks were wet. "We have to report to the office tomorrow. I was hoping to say goodbye to Blue."

"Oh," Molly's own pain wouldn't let her move but Kelly's made her stand to wrap her arms around them. "I'll step outside with Tom while you say what you need to."

"Are you sure?" Kelly whispered.

"Of course," Molly gave them a last squeeze. "The cop doesn't want us talking about after Blue was grabbed but anything else is fair game."

***

Darkness gave way to a fog as if his mind were filled with glue but Blue was used to waking with no memories — it was the reason he drank.

Someone held his hand. Memory swam like a fish

through the murk.

"Molly?" His voice rasped as if he'd been swallowing sand.

"Molly's outside. She'll be back soon."

Another larger fish.

"A car accident..." Blue tried to move. "I'm in the hospital. Kelly!"

"I'm here."

He tried to focus but his eyes wouldn't cooperate. A minnow flashed and was gone.

"I have to go back to the office."

Wet drops splashed on Blue's hand.

"Kelly, did you say you think you loved me?"

"I did."

"What did I say?" Blue tried to chase a minnow, but an ominous shape chased it away.

"That you'd be here when I figured it out."

"Sounds like something I'd say," Blue turned his attention to the lurking giant at the edges of his mind.

***

Molly sat up as the door opened. Kelly came out looking fragile. She walked over and wrapped her arms around them.

"All you need to do is be still. Ciara taught me this."

Kelly froze, then slowly relaxed and put their arms around Molly. They stood in silence while Molly's heart beat steadily.

"Tell Ciara thanks for me." Kelly spoke into Molly's ear, then stepped back.

"I will," Molly pulled the phone from her purse.

"You'll need this back."

"You can keep it. IT already wiped all the company programs from it before I gave it to you, or it would have got me fired. They've disabled the connection to the company network so now it is just a phone with extra-strength encryption for your files." Kelly smiled. "We left something for you at home. I wasn't sure we'd connect before we had to catch our flight. Call me and let me know what you think."

"I will."

"Jack asked me to tell you that if you ever want to get into security to talk to him." Tom shook her hand.

"I will keep it in mind if social work doesn't pan out."

"His card." Tom placed a card with a phone number and nothing else on it on the table beside Molly's chair. "He doesn't give out many of these. Keep it safe."

He grinned at her, "I get the feeling we'll be seeing you again."

Kelly waved one last time and they vanished down the hall. Molly put the card carefully in her pocket and went back to sit with Blue.

Chapter 24

Wednesday, June 23

Molly groaned and stretched out the kinks in her back. "I told you to go home to sleep," Blue's eyes twinkled at her.

"You were also talking about fish in your head."

"Right!" Blue pushed himself more upright in the bed. "Maybe I'll get to go home..." He trailed off and put his hand to his head. "I don't have a home anymore, do I?"

"As long as I'm alive, you will have a home with me," Molly pointed at him.

"That's good to hear, as long as Martha doesn't toss you out when she meets me."

"She's looking forward to meeting you."

A knock at the door interrupted them.

Constable Madoc smiled at them. "Constable Post told me you were here. I thought I'd drop in and say hello,"

"Come in," Blue motioned to her. He took a sip of water. "Still tastes like smoke."

"How are you feeling?" She sat in the chair Molly had vacated, 'I've heard you've been having a rough time."

"The last thing I remember clearly is going off the road in a car. The rest is like someone took half the puzzle pieces and scattered the rest on the floor. I may have to accept that most of a week is gone and probably won't come back."

"That could be tough." Madoc leaned forward, "We

all like to think we can rely on our memories."

"I used to think there were memories I had to get rid of. Now there are memories I want back," Blue shrugged. "I expect Sam would say I've made one step forward, now take the next one."

"What would that be?" Madoc tilted her head slightly.

"Damned if I know!" Blue laughed, then coughed, "That was what he said."

"Wise man," Madoc chuckled.

"Or a wise ass — there isn't much distance between them."

Blue drank his water.

The doctor came in and peered at Blue, "Your blood oxygen is good. I've written you a script for meds. Some are for pain; others to deal with the burns in your throat and airway."

"Is that why everything tastes like smoke?" Blue asked.

"No, that would be from the fires surrounding us turning half the province to ashes." Molly's face reddened as the doctor and Blue looked at her.

"She's not far off." The doctor looked back to Blue. "Take the medication as prescribed and if you get worse, come straight back in. Smoke inhalation can be tricky at times. For now, there is no reason why you can't go home."

"Best news I've heard all day," Blue swung to sit on the edge of the bed, "but what am I supposed to wear? All my clothes are ashes."

***

With help from Bobbie Molly got clothes for Blue. Then they took him to Martha's and got him installed in a room.

"Martha says you can use this blue room — unless you'd prefer the pink one?

"Nothing wrong with pink but the blue is more relaxing." Blue lay down on the bed and sighed, "It's going to take me time to get back to normal. I haven't had cravings for booze this hard in ages."

"We'll work it through," Molly sat on the edge of the bed beside him.

"Thanks." Blue closed his eyes. "Think I'm going to get some napping in."

Molly left him resting and went to talk to Martha who sat in the kitchen as she did most of the time.

"How is he doing, dear?"

"Sleeping." Molly sat with a sigh. "I'm not sure what we're going to do next. As much I love staying with you, it feels more like staying in a hotel. It isn't my place."

"That's what I'm afraid of if I move," Martha tapped her cane. "With this, I can put my hand on everything I need without hesitation. I've learned this house over the decades."

Molly tried to imagine that.

"But you know it was so much fun meeting with the Pointy Shoes, and you've been a darling. Maybe I should think about going somewhere I can live with people again. I'll miss this but if all I'm doing is sitting in the kitchen…"

"Trusting Blue was one of the hardest things I've ever done but now I can't imagine not trusting him," Molly got up and put the kettle on.

"People need change but we also hate it," Martha laughed. "I missed our comfortable little place when we moved in here. I'll miss this place too but better to move while I'm still able to adapt to a new place."

"When are you thinking of moving?" Molly's heart sank, though she agreed with Martha.

"I'm on a waiting list. It's a private home but they said it could be a month or six months. They have a respite bed if I want to go and try it out."

"That sounds like a good idea," Molly heated the teapot, then added the bag and boiling water. She put the chicken tea cozy on it while she laid out the cups and saucers.

"There should be a few cookies left on a plate in the fridge."

Molly put the plate on the table and sat in her chair.

"You aren't asking me." Martha turned her face toward Molly

"Asking what?".

"Where are you going to live."

Molly smiled as she poured the tea, "Blue and I will find a place. I have no doubt about that."

Chapter 25

Tuesday, August 19

In their new apartment, Molly laid out the cups for tea. Hanna and Ciara were coming over to celebrate Ciara's acceptance into the choir at TRU. Martha had insisted that Molly take the pot, the cozy and four of the cups and saucers.

The Pointy Shoes had helped her and Blue find an apartment. They ended up on the North Shore again, on Fortune. The bus to the university stopped just out front and Northhills Mall was an easy walk.

They never did get any money from the motel. It closed for a month, then re-opened under new management. Dusi told her it was a different woman at the counter. A very friendly Vietnamese woman who, since coming to Canada in the '70s, had been saving up to buy a motel. Her family had a hotel in Saigon and her son had taken Dusi on a tour.

Constable Post had said the case was pushed off the priority list. The apartments were boarded up with warning signs plastered all over them.

Someone knocked at the door and Molly sighed. She wished people wouldn't let others in. Picking up her cell, she dialled 911, but didn't hit 'connect'. Then she peered through the peephole in the door, Ciara was bouncing on her toes. The tension drained from Molly's shoulders and she closed the phone app.

"Welcome!" Molly grinned as she opened the door, "Congratulations, Ciara!"

"I'm not sure that her feet have touched the ground since the audition," Hanna tugged on Ciara's braid. "The director gave her some lessons on the spot, so it was more like a class than an audition."

"Mr. Josiah heard me sing in June. He liked my songs."

Molly brought them to the tiny table which acted as the transition from the kitchen to the living room.

"Molly, these cups are beautiful," Hanna looked over at her.

"Martha made me promise to use them and not put them on a shelf. I trust Ciara with them." Molly winked and took a plate from the cupboard to put cookies on it. Then she put the water on to boil, "I'd love to tell you I baked these myself, but I bought them at the grocery store."

Hanna laughed and sat down after getting Ciara to sit. The girl touched the cups like she wasn't sure they were real.

"Cookies are cookies," Ciara picked up one to nibble on.

"Tea will be ready in a minute."

"I didn't think you'd be the china teacup type," Hanna lifted one to examine it closely.

Molly brought the tea pot over with its chicken cozy.

"It doesn't really go with the china, does it?" Molly grinned. "Martha's granddaughter made it for her years ago. It didn't matter how it looks if it keeps the tea warm."

"I like it." Ciara ran her fingers down the beak.

After pouring the tea and adding milk and sugar for Ciara, Molly sat down and sighed,

"I would never have thought such a simple thing would be so satisfying."

"Hospitality is always important," Hanna sipped at the tea. "Too many have forgotten that. My mother would have used her last bit of tea to serve a guest, even a stranger."

"It tastes better in this cup," Ciara held the cup with great care.

"How is Blue doing?" Hanna glanced at Ciara who paid no attention to the adult conversation.

"He's been going to AA two or three times a week. Says it may not be his fault he went on a binge but it is his responsibility to get help to prevent it happening again."

"Good for him!" Hanna raised her teacup, "And what about you?"

"I went to NA while in Alberta, and once things settled down here, I went to a few to build a relationship with the group. Once a month is good for now and they're ready if I need them more often. I've been asked to sponsor someone — still thinking about that."

"You'd be good at it," Hanna took a cookie. "Ciara is right: a cookie is a cookie."

As they were leaving, Ciara pointed to Molly's purse hanging on the hook by the door, "I know who made that. She came to school one time to teach us beading."

"A friend gave it to me to match the dress."

"It does that!" Hanna ran her fingers along the beading. "That reminds me, I have something else to talk to you about when you're ready."

"How will I know I'm ready if I don't know what it's about?" Molly hugged Ciara then Hanna.

"You'll figure it out," Hanna gave Molly an extra squeeze before herding Ciara out the door.

***

Blue came in to find Molly holding her purse and looking deep in thought.

"What's up? You look like the answer to the world's problems is hidden in there."

"Hanna looked at this and said it reminded her that she wanted to talk to me about something when I was ready."

"And now you're wondering what she wants to talk about."

"Wouldn't you?"

"Of course!" Blue set a pot of water on to boil, took a bag of spaghetti sauce from the freezer and dropped it in a bowl to microwave, "But talking about getting ready for things, when do your courses start?"

"In about three weeks. Orientation is the week after Labour Day. I didn't think one of my first courses would be statistics — I hate math!"

"Never liked it much myself." Blue put bowls on the table and dropped spaghetti in the pot. "Some salad in the fridge from last night — maybe grab it out."

"Sure thing." Molly hung the purse up in its place and helped with the dinner preparations.

Later in the evening, as Molly was snorting at videos on Youtube, Blue answered a call from Kelly.

"How's it going?" he asked.

"Busy as usual," Kelly scrubbed at their eyes. "Anything come back?"

"No, nothing after going off the road." Blue leaned forward, "I wish I could remember. They feel like important memories."

"They are," Kelly looked away from the phone camera, "But it doesn't feel real if you don't remember. Maybe I made up your response."

"There's only one way to find out," Blue wasn't sure what he felt, but something connected him to this person.

"I'm scared," Kelly didn't look at the camera. "I've never felt anything like this before. How do I know it's real?"

"Maybe it doesn't matter so much about whether it was real before as much as if it is real now."

"I don't know, I'd better go."

"I'm here when you need me," Blue said but she probably didn't hear it.

He lay on the bed and stared at the ceiling. The craving for alcohol didn't feel like his own, but he had to deal with it. The idea that someone had grabbed him, drugged him, and forced him to drink made him sick. Kelly's struggle with what was real, resonated with him. All he could do was act as if the cravings were real and get them under control.

At least he'd been able to go back to work. Whatever happened had released, or repressed, the trauma from the fire. It wasn't just about Kelly. Nothing else made sense, even what he *could* remember.

Rod and Harley had left the motel without giving a forwarding address. Since Rod had paid his bill, the management wasn't worried about it, but Blue missed Harley

Simon had gone too. He had a job and a tiny apartment. Blue had a hard time getting his head around that. It was like the world had shifted somehow and left him behind.

Chapter 26

Friday, August 22

Molly went for a walk over to Rivers Trail and headed north to work out the tangle in her head. She was worried about Blue. On the surface, he looked fine and sounded like he always had.

But that gap in his memory was eating at him, she was sure of it. Too often he stared into space, forehead furrowed. The problem wasn't the abduction. It was Kelly. He'd lost important memories and probably felt like it was his fault somehow.

Molly kicked a stone out of her way. It bothered her that he'd been trapped somewhere and she hadn't found him. Her heart equated that with failure. He'd been there for her, but she'd fallen short.

Then there was Hanna. What could she want to talk about? Ciara was her normal bubbly self, and except for that one brief discussion, Hanna had been completely normal too.

At the soccer field, Molly's foot began to ache. It looked like a normal foot but there was damage underneath from when she'd been grabbed which made itself known when she pushed too hard.

She'd passed a bench not too far back. Molly walked back to sit on it.

The day was warm but the breeze off the river kept her comfortable, so she settled in to watch the river. People walked, rode, skateboarded, and ran in both directions — many of them accompanied by dogs.

The more relaxed walkers said a word or two as they passed. Others moved like they were alone in the world. To her disbelief, a young man in dark glasses with a red and white cane, talking on a cell phone, skateboarded past her.

A cold nose nudged her and Molly scratched the dog before recognizing Harley. The dog looked at her with a goofy grin. A shrill whistle sounded, and Harley took off at a full run. Molly admired the strength of the dog. A figure that might have been Rod met the dog and walked off the path.

When he'd talked to her at the outlook, Molly hadn't been scared but filled with sadness. She'd encountered so many people who made her life look like fun. The interest in social work was to understand how humans could damage each other so badly as well as help the damaged ones.

Her mind went back to Hanna and her strange comment. Maybe it had something to do with Ciara declaring Molly an aunt, but she could imagine why the need to be ready.

What if being ready didn't have anything to do with the content of the conversation? Was Molly ready to listen regardless of what she'd learn?

Molly shivered and realized she'd been sitting much longer than she'd planned. A few steps told her the ache in her foot had faded enough to get home.

As Molly walked, she pulled out her cellphone and dialled Hanna's number.

"Hello," Ciara answered. "Sorry, grandma can't come to the phone so leave a message and she'll get back to you. And if you're calling for me, tell grandma I should have my own phone."

Molly laughed.

"Ciara, I'm sure you'd love your own phone but I'm staying out of that discussion. Hanna, I've been thinking about what you said. I'm ready to hear whatever it is you have to say. I can't imagine anything you need to say that I can't handle with some help."

Instead of putting the phone back in her pocket, Molly carried it in her hand in case Hanna called back. She hated the frantic feel of scrabbling to answer the phone before it went to voicemail.

Two men dressed in chinos and long-sleeved polo shirts stepped out from the park as if they'd been waiting for her. Molly's hackles went up and she picked up her pace. They stayed the same distance back and she wondered if she was getting paranoid.

She and Blue were normal people now. Who would want to grab her?

When an older couple with two dogs passed heading in the other direction, Molly almost turned and followed them.

Don't be silly. It's the middle of the day.. A 'good afternoon' and a muttered reply came to her and Molly relaxed more.

The phone rang and she almost dropped it.

"Hi," Molly slowed down to talk.

"Grandma's at a meeting," Ciara said. "She told me I could ask people about the phone but most are like you. I think she knew that."

"Probably."

"I will tell her to call…"

Molly missed the rest of Ciara's sentence as a man in a suit and tie stepped out in front of her from under the Halston bridge.

"I knew I'd find you, girl. You don't know how much money you're costing me."

She didn't recognize him until his eyes fixed on hers, George.

"What do you want?" Molly swivelled to keep an eye on the men behind her.

"I'm going to take my money back out of your skin," his smile was cold and predatory.

The other two were closing in, no time to hesitate. Molly darted forward, her body remembering the drills. George grinned and held his hands out. She shifted her attack slightly to use the extra leverage of his arm to take him down as hard as she could. A black car waited by the yellow gate, so Molly bolted down to the beach.

"Get the fucking bitch!" George yelled. "Forget snatching her — kill her and toss her in the river."

Molly thought to call for help but she'd dropped her phone under the bridge. She put her energy into running. Of course, the beach was deserted.

The gravel dragged at her feet and she staggered, so she crawled up the slope to the path and kept running. The guys behind were yelling something but Molly didn't care. She saved her breath for running.

Usually, a short sprint got her out of whatever trouble

threatened, but this was the second time her flight became a long-distance run. Her chest hurt, and air came and went in painful gasps.

A police car pulled out onto Schubert and Molly aimed for it, waving her hands. The car stopped but she couldn't, so she hit the front and rolled over the hood to fall on the road. Her head banged on the pavement and white pain flared in her mind.

A weight landed on her back, then her arms were twisted painfully behind her back. The cold of cuffs snapped brutally tight on her wrists.

"This is a nice neighbourhood — no place for people like you," Rough hands lifted her and slammed her down again. Molly's nose crunched and she screamed.

"What is going on?" a new voice boomed.

"I'm making an arrest — what does it look like?"

"A stupid ass guy who doesn't care about making cops look bad." The voice yelled at someone else, "Don't you move! Piss me off and I won't be as gentle as this asshole. Get down and stay down."

Hands picked up Molly and pushed her against the car.

"Touch her again and I'll charge you with assault."

"Stay out of it, Post."

"Do you even listen to the radio? After our call about a girl stealing a wallet and bolting, dispatch reported that a call had been cut off when threats were heard in the background to 'kill her'. Then more calls came in saying two goons were chasing a young Native woman."

Gentler hands lifted Molly from the hood and undid the cuffs.

"Don't mess with me — I can make your life fucking miserable."

"My radio is still broadcasting, moron. Shut up before you dig yourself out of a job," Molly peered at Constable Post through the blood dripping off her forehead. He still looked cold and unapproachable.

The other cop jumped into his cruiser.

"Supervisor's on the way," Post waved at the two zip-tied on the path. "You watch those boys, or cut them loose, but look at the gang tats before you make assumptions. Damn! It's assholes like you who make my job harder."

Post guided Molly to his cruiser and spoke into his radio.

"I'm taking the young woman to the hospital for treatment," he said as he threw his car into gear and drove off, leaving a crowd with open mouths watching the scene.

"Why?" Molly whispered. It hurt to talk as her jaw was swelling fast.

"It's my job," Post didn't look at her. "The shitty part is when I have to protect people from other cops."

"Thanks. Could you call Blue and tell him what happened?"

Post talked into his radio but Molly picked up only one word in three.

The radio squawked as they pulled up in front of Emerg. Post frowned, "He isn't answering his phone."

Molly's heart dropped. "Drop me off and go look for him, please."

"I'm walking you in first," Post parked, walked around and helped her out of the car.

People talked around her, but Molly didn't listen. She clung to consciousness as if staying awake was the only thing that could save Blue.

Chapter 27

Blue was walking home from work when he got the text from Molly

"Saw something strange at the old apartment. Meet you there."

"Ok...on my way."

Blue sighed. He wanted nothing more than to go home and relax on the couch. As he walked, Blue reflected on what Molly might have seen. The place was boarded up tight. Maybe some of the boards were missing but would she really want him to look at something like that?

He texted her.

"What's up?"

No response so he phoned her, and it went straight to the answering machine. His gut knotted — something wasn't right. He strode along faster. The only way to know if she was in trouble was to go to the apartment.

Blue stared at his phone, then phoned 911. When he got through to Kamloops dispatch he told them he'd seen kids breaking into the apartments and reminded them it was a toxic site. The woman dispatcher said she'd put it out on the radio, and someone would swing by to check it out.

"Great — sometime after shift change!" He'd done what he could to get backup, now the rest was up to him.

Blue cut through the back streets to get to the alley without being seen on Tranquille. The signs were lurid in their warnings the place was toxic, but he didn't see any gaps or openings.

Columbia Smoke

The alley was deserted. If this was a movie, he'd be rolling his eyes at the foolishness of the character. Instead, he looked for any sign of Molly. A hedge ran between the parking spaces in the back and the building, providing a bit of a shield between the second floor apartments and the alley. Graffiti covered the plywood, most of it the 'Look at me — I was here' variety.

Something growled at his side and Blue looked down to see Harley.

"So that's how it is, girl?"

Harley herded him behind the hedge. Maybe it was Blue's imagination, but she didn't look happy.

Rod waited for him, cell phone in hand.

"Please don't do anything stupid — I don't want to make Harley bite you," he lifted the phone to his mouth, "...he's here."

"It's been a while Rod."

"I told him to leave well enough alone, but your girl pissed him off."

"Smart people aren't in this business." Blue scratched Harley behind her ears and she gave a half growl/half whine.

"You set the fire?" Blue crouched down to scratch Harley more.

"No. I told Wanda how to do it. All she needed was to wait a month, then leave, but she wanted to be important."

"You killed her?"

"That was George's thugs. I don't like to get involved directly, I'm more of a ... consultant."

"Molly told me what you'd said."

207

"Of course she did. Perhaps I foolishly looked for understanding."

"Don't we all?" Blue sighed and went back to scratching Harley.

"Stop touching my dog," Rod held a gun in his hand, "Harley, come."

The dog crouched and whined but refused to move, blocking most of Blue's body.

Rod's face twisted and Blue saw emotion on it for the first time; not anger but grief.

"I should have never talked to you. Right from the beginning, you've been stealing my dog."

"Not deliberately." Blue pushed at the dog. "Go to your master." She twisted her head to look at him but refused to move.

"What's your problem?" A man in a suit stepped through the hedge, gun pointed between Rod and Blue. He leered at Blue, "By now that little girl you're shacked up with is floating in the river. I was going to sell her, but she ticked me off. You two cost me a lot of money, lost the motel and the apartment."

"A smart man would cut his losses and start up somewhere else," Blue shrugged and stood up. "So, of course you stayed around for revenge." His heart ached. At the end, he'd let Molly down. Time to let it go. *Kelly.* He couldn't understand why the thought of them pulled at his heart.

Harley stood between Blue and the man with her hackles up, growling in a way that made Blue wonder how the guy wasn't wetting his pants.

"Damned dog." He aimed at Harley.

"No!" Rod jumped on the guy's arm, apparently forgetting he held a gun in his own hand.

A shot echoed off the apartment and Rod staggered back. The guy aimed at Rod again.

Harley snarled and lunged at the guy. She bit his arm and shook him. The gun banged and the dog fell to the ground as the guy took the gun in his left hand, blood streaming down his right arm. Blue ran over to Rod.

Whether the guy intended to shoot Harley, Rod, or Blue wasn't clear, it didn't matter.

"Take care of Harley," Rod lifted his gun and shot the guy through the heart, "Asshole!" He dropped his hand on the ground.

Blue ran over to Harley. She whimpered as he checked where she was hurt. The bullet had shattered her right front leg.

"Damn!" Constable Post stepped cautiously around the end of the hedge. "Two gunshot wounds. Neither one looks good," he spoke into his radio.

"Harley needs help," Blue looked up from where he was trying to stem the flow of blood.

"Need immediate transport for an injured dog," Post looked around and relaxed a little. Neither Rod nor the guy, looked to be breathing. Blue would mourn Rod, for Harley's sake, the man was walking wounded like so many people.

"Your girl, Molly — she's at the hospital — a bit bruised up but nothing lethal."

It felt like Blue's heart started beating again. "Thanks," Harley licked his hand, "Thank you."

Chapter 28

Sunday, August 24

Molly jumped up as Blue walked into their apartment carrying Harley.

"The vet said she's doing well. She can move about but not to let her push it too far. She'll go back in a month for a checkup."

"The poor girl. I wonder how she'll adapt to having only three legs."

"I don't think it will slow Harley down. She's a survivor — like someone else I know," Blue put the dog on the bed Molly had bought for her. Harley looked around, then put her head down to sleep. "When are Hanna and Ciara arriving?"

"In just a few minutes. Your timing was good."

"Are you good with this?" Blue sat down close to Harley.

"Nothing she can tell me will change who I am and I'm curious, more than nervous, about it," Molly perched on a chair at their little dining table and tried to look relaxed.

Blue raised an eyebrow at her.

"Ok — I am nervous, but I'm more curious," she admitted as she leaped up when someone knocked at the door. After checking the peephole, Molly let them in.

"You haven't met Harley yet. She's an extraordinary dog but she just got back from the vet a few minutes ago, so you'll have to wait until another time to meet her properly."

"She's got only three legs!" Ciara's eyes widened.

"Her front leg was shattered by a bullet while she was saving Blue's life."

"Wow!" Ciara's eyes went even wider.

"Come on...I have the water boiling for tea, and cookies I made myself so they might not be as good as the last batch."

"Cookies are cookies," Ciara sat at the table and admired the cups again. "Can I use a different one today?"

"Choose whichever one you want."

When the four of them were sitting around the table, teacups filled, cookies in hand, Molly took a deep breath.

"Ok, Hanna. I'm ready."

"I was surprised you wanted Ciara here," Hanna glanced over at her granddaughter.

"Ciara's a friend. Without her, we'd never have met."

"Very well then," Hanna smiled at Ciara as the girl beamed. "You saw how Bobbie and I were. She was the Child and Family Services worker for many years. While I'm sure she worked very hard at doing the best job she could, she didn't know anything about our people and wasn't interested in learning. For her, families were families, and the same measuring stick could be used for everyone. We butted heads constantly. I worked in the Band Office and knew everyone whose lives were changed by CFS intervention, and that was a lot of us."

Hanna drank some tea as she visibly fought for control.

Columbia Smoke

"A cousin of mine, Rose, was especially hard hit. CFS took away her three youngest children. My cousin was troubled but the community was there for her. We had our own way of dealing with such things," her eyes flickered over to where Ciara listened and was taking it all in.

"She was left with only her daughter who was sixteen at the time, mostly because the girl refused any notion of any involvement with CFS. Bobbie kept visiting. She thought of it as checking in but my family and friends experienced it as harassment.

"Then, without warning, Rose's daughter ran away to Vancouver. Rose searched for her, Even asked Bobbie to get the CFS to help but the girl had vanished." Hanna wiped her eyes with her napkin, "Six months later Rose had a visit from the RCMP. They said her daughter had jumped from a bridge and drowned. That was September 14, 1998."

Molly's hand was shaking so much that she had to put her teacup down.

"Months later, we heard from the coroner that the girl had just given birth very recently; within days of her suicide. Rose got worse then, with no one to live for, and died a year or so later. I never did find out anything about the other three children. I wasn't a direct relative, so CFS wouldn't tell me anything."

Hanna looked into her teacup as if it held an answer to the tragedy, "The daughter's name was Molly. You look a lot like her." She took a photo from her pocket and slid it over to Molly. It showed a thin girl, eyes filled with pain yet still challenging the camera.

"She..." Molly couldn't find the words but touched the photo. The cheekbones were the same as the ones she saw in the mirror every day.

"Molly, the very last thing your mother did in her life was to make sure you'd survive. Somehow they gave you her name."

Molly's tears flowed down her cheeks and splashed on the photograph.

"All these years, I've hated you Mom."

Blue's arms went around her and held her as Molly sobbed, clutching the photograph.

When she could talk, Molly looked at Hanna, "You gave me Mom's love back. I don't know what to say."

"You don't have to say anything." Hanna took Molly's hand, "Let it sink in. From the very beginning, you were loved. Your mother was a fighter, and got into all kinds of trouble. Someday, I'll tell you some stories about her.

"I would like that."

Ciara stood up and started singing with Hanna quietly joining her. Though Molly didn't understand the words, the music flowed like a balm through her heart.

"That's Mother Earth's song," Ciara said when she'd finished and sat down.

"Thank you," Molly stared at the photo and daubed at it.

"I can get another copy made," Hanna said.

"No, the tears stains are part of the picture. They connect me and Mom somehow." Molly looked up at Hanna suddenly. "You said she had brothers and sisters?"

"Yes. I don't know any more than that, but Bobbie said

she'd help you get permission to search."

"You talked to Bobbie?"

"She was part of the story too: not quite a villain; not quite a hero. For years she's tried to find some way of making up for the inadvertent damage she did. This is something, a beginning."

Molly studied the picture again, "I thought nothing you could tell me would change who I am, and it hasn't. But it has. The beginning is new. I wasn't trash." Molly held the photo to her heart.

***

Blue sat in his room waiting for Kelly's call. Molly had bought a frame for her mother's picture and had it on her bedside table. She was probably still looking at it.

The computer beeped and Blue connected the call.

"Hi, Kelly!"

"How are you doing after Friday's excitement?"

"It wasn't the first time someone's wanted to kill me." Blue leaned back, "It wasn't personal, at least not for me. It was about the guy's ego, not really about me. The harder part is Rod. I can't say we were friends, but we were more than acquaintances. I was the one he trusted to care for Harley."

"What about the apartment — how did they react to you suddenly having a big, black dog?"

"We negotiated and arrived at a mutual agreement. The building isn't 'no pets'. They do allow smaller dogs, but they made an exception for me. Harley's a bit of a celebrity at the moment. The apartment block owner is local and liked the idea of a connection to Harley. She wanted to say Harley was my emotional support dog even though that doesn't carry any weight legally. I told her I was Harley's emotional support human!"

Kelly laughed. They hadn't laughed much before.

"Look Kelly, I did some thinking. I don't think we're going anywhere this way. I'm not going to get those memories back. To me, it is a nice story but not something I can connect to."

Kelly's face fell and Blue held up his hand.

"I don't have the memories, but the feelings are still here," he tapped his chest. "I don't want to worry about what is gone. Let's work on what we have."

"What do we have?" Kelly leaned forward.

"The hell if I know, but the only way to find out is to move forward."

"Forward?"

"I'd like you to visit here or I'll come to you. We'll make new memories, though if we can avoid the car crash, I'd appreciate it."

"I would like that very much; the visiting, and the avoiding the car crash. I've never done anything like this."

"Neither have I," Blue shrugged and leaned closer to the computer. "We'll make it up as we go along."

"I have some time off next weekend," Kelly looked down, blushing. "If you don't mind, I can stay in a hotel."

"How about we decide that when you get here? We have real furniture now, so there's a sofa I can sleep on," Blue leaned back again. "Molly's talked about painting the walls and she has chosen the furniture. We didn't buy just whatever was cheap. The Pointy Shoes ladies made her go through their garages and junk rooms too, so there are even pictures on the wall."

"Sounds nice," Kelly smiled. "How is Molly doing? You said she got beat up again."

"She just shrugs off physical things like that. That she didn't ride to my rescue was bugging her, but Friday's events reminded her we have limits to what we can do. That doesn't mean she won't crash into those limits and try to push through them."

"So she's going to be okay?"

"More than okay. You won't believe what she found out today…"

***

Blue went out to the living room to check on Harley. She licked his hand as he carried her outside to do her business.

Once back in the apartment Blue lay down on the couch with Harley's dog bed close by.

"What do you think, Harley? Is all this going to work?"

Harley licked his hand again, then bumped it until he scratched her behind the ears. She gave a huge sigh then flopped on her bed with Blue's hand on her head.

Blue closed his eyes. "Yeah, I think you're right."

About the Author

Alex has been writing books for decades and has published twenty-five books. He is a member of the Lived Experience Committee out of the LOOP. This is his second Blue in Kamloops novel.

He lives in Kamloops with his dog and scotch collection and fights cage matches with the stories in his head to decide what will get written next.

Other books by Alex

Series:

Calliope Books
Calliope and the Sea Serpent
Calliope and the Royal Engineers
The Third Prince and the Enemy's Daughter
Calliope and the Khirshan Empire

Spruce Bay Books
Wendigo Whispers
Cry of the White Moose
Disputed Rock

The Belandria Tarot
The Devil Reversed
The Regent's Reign
The Empire Unbalanced
The World Widens
The Fury Unleashed

Blue in Kamloops
Tranquille Dark
Columbia Smoke

Alex McGilvery

Stand alone books:

Generation Gap
The Gods Above
Tales of Light and Dark
Like Mushrooms (poetry and photography)
The Heronmaster
Blood and Sparkles, and other stories
Princess of Boring
By the Book
Sarcasm is My Superpower
Playing on Yggdrasil
The Unenchanted Princess

Read short stories and excerpts from his novels at alexmcgilvery.com

Printed in the USA
CPSIA information can be obtained
at www.ICGtesting.com
JSHW021211150923
48203JS00004B/100